REANIMATOR TALES:
THE GREWSOME ADVENTURES
OF HERBERT WEST
&
SUPERNATURAL HORROR
IN LITERATURE

CALIBER
BOOKS

REANIMATOR TALES:
THE GREWSOME ADVENTURES OF HERBERT WEST
&
SUPERNATURAL HORROR IN LITERATURE

By
H. P. LOVECRAFT

EDITED & ORIGINAL MATERIAL BY
Steven Philip Jones

FOREWORD BY
Justin Beahm

CALIBER ENTERTAINMENT
www.calibercomics.com

The text of *Supernatural Horror in Literature* is taken from the edition prepared by S. T. Joshi (New York: Hippocampus Press, 2000, 2012) and is used with his permission.

Supernatural Horror in Literature appears here with the permission of Lovecraft Holdings, L.L.C.

The text for "From the Dark," "The Plague-Daemon," "Six Shots by Moonlight," "The Scream of the Dead," "The Horror from the Shadows" and "The Tomb-Legions" originally appeared in *Re-Animator: Tales of Herbert West* (Malibu Graphics, 1991).

Introduction, "The Empty House on Harley Street," Audio Script for "From the Dark," and all editorial material © 2015 by Steven Philip Jones

Foreword © 2014 by Justin Beahm

Interior Illustrations © 2016 by Terry Pavlet

Cover Art by Nabetse Zitro

First Edition

.

To Peter Cushing & Terence Fisher
S.P.J.

CONTENTS

ILLUSTRATIONS

Interior illustrations by Terry Pavlet

Cover Art by Nabetse Zitro

FOREWORD

Hearing Steven Philip Jones talk about Lovecraft is akin to lifting the flap on a canvas tent and settling in for a revival sermon. His love for the man inspires, and calls into check the passion of anyone within earshot. Think you know all things wet and dastardly? Think again. As such, there is no one better to helm a tome such as this. You are in good hands, dear reader.

Like Howard Phillips, Steven Philip grew up fascinated by beasties and ghouls, a curiosity that informed his exploration of print and cinema and helped him find his voice in written word. Consideration of, and for, what may lurk in the ether led Jones on myriad adventures, from radio to comics and beyond, and throughout, he made regular pilgrimages back to the fertile land first charted by Lovecraft.

As such, this is something of a homecoming for one of Iowa's literary treasures, as well as the celebration of one of the key figures in modern literature. Two men courting the fantastic, separated by eras yet bound by a common compulsion. Without dexterous storytellers, myth is lost to the thief of time, which is why volumes like this are so important.

You hear that noise at the door? Some immense slippery body lumbering against it? Fear not, for you have the best guide this drafty old house has to offer, and that thing surely won't get in.

Will it?

Justin Beahm
March 10, 2014

INTRODUCTION

Since 1985 most people have been introduced to Dr. Herbert West in the movie *Re-Animator* starring Jeffrey Combs, which made West a cult figure and horror icon, but it all started with H. P. Lovecraft and an almost forgotten series he wrote called *Grewsome Tales*. If you are unfamiliar with the gentleman author from Rhode Island, H(oward) P(hillips) Lovecraft, let me offer a few highlights from his life up to 1921 when he created West. (Please feel free to skip ahead if you are already schooled on this.)

Lovecraft was born August 20, 1890 in Providence, his home for most of his life and his first and best love. In 1893 Lovecraft and his mother Sarah Susan Phillips moved in with his grandfather Whipple V. Phillips after his father, Winfield Scott Lovecraft, was declared insane and committed to Butler Hospital where he died (possibly of syphilis)[1] in 1898. Whipple Phillips died in 1904, which forced Sarah and her son to move to a nearby apartment where they fell into a life of genteel poverty. The popular image of Lovecraft is that he was a neurotic and bookish child who grew up to be a neurotic and bookish recluse pining for the days of 18th-century British conservatism, but by Lovecraft's own admission he "behaved like any active, sociable American boy, as normal as Tom Sawyer or Penrod," taking long bike rides in the country, waging wars in the woods as a member of the "Salter Avenue Army," and smoking tobacco behind the stables even though he detested the stuff.[2] That said, headaches, anxieties, and maybe a nervous breakdown prevented Lovecraft from graduating high school, and between 1908 and 1913 Lovecraft withdrew from the world, staying mostly at home with the overprotective Sarah. In 1914, though, he joined the United Amateur Press Association and began several correspondences with new friends, many of whom he would eventually travel to meet. By 1917 Lovecraft felt up to volunteering for the Rhode Island National Guard, which gave him a physical and a clean bill of health, although Sarah managed to squelch his enlistment. Two years later Sarah was institutionalized and committed to Butler Hospital where she died in 1922. That same year a UAP friend, George Houtain, made Lovecraft a professional writer by paying five dollars an episode for *Grewsome Tales* and publishing it in *Home Brew*, "America's Zippiest Pocket Magazine" which specialized in "Peppy Stories – Pungent Jests – Piquant Gossip." *Grewsome Tales* ran from February to July.

* * *

Now "America's Zippiest Magazine" may not sound like a publication where you would find a typical Lovecraft weird story, much less a series about a deranged doctor and increasingly apprehensive associate scrounging for cadavers to resurrect, but Houtain got what he asked for from Lovecraft in *Grewsome Tales*[3] and even proclaimed its fifth installment as "Better than Edgar Allan Poe" on the June 1922 cover.[4] (Spoiler alert: it ain't.) On the other hand *Grewsome Tales*, or *Herbert West - Reanimator* as the series is called today, is not a typical Lovecraft story.

First it *is* a series, one of only two written by Lovecraft.[5]

Second, Herbert West is Lovecraft's only continuing series character.[6] Each *Grewsome Tales* episode features one in a series of adventures about West and his associate, the series' anonymous Narrator, from 1903 to 1920.[7] In contrast each episode of Lovecraft's other series "The Lurking Fear" (1923) is about the unraveling of a ghastly series of murders in the Catskill Mountains over a period of a few days.

Third, *Grewsome Tales* may not be so out of place in a zippy magazine. Its six episodes are hardly comedic,[8] however there is dark and indelicate tongue-in-cheek humor sprinkled throughout, though nothing that distracts from the series' horrific moments.

Fourth and finally, Houtain dictated that each installment be no longer than two thousand words, giving Lovecraft little room to operate.[9] Most Lovecraft stories emphasize atmosphere, which he explains is crucial to horror literature in his groundbreaking literary treatise *Supernatural Horror in Literature* (1927, 1933-4);[10] however atmosphere, like its sneaky evil twin suspense, generally requires time for a young writer to develop. Lovecraft eventually mastered the art of conjuring atmosphere in a few words or sentences,[11] but in *Grewsome Tales* he often resorts to hyping each episode's gore[12] and Gothic elements.

But *what* gore and Gothic elements!

Lovecraft complained while writing *Grewsome Tales* that he had been reduced to a Grub Street hack,[13] but Lovecraft scholar S. T. Joshi suggests that he might have "got a kick out of this literary slumming,"[14] and Lovecraft does appear to revel in West's unnatural experiments. Almost every adventure grows wilder than the last until West's "scientific zeal" degenerates "to an unhealthy and fantastic mania" that becomes "fiendishly disgusting[.]" This megalomanic descent is also the arc or plot point that drives and unifies *Grewsome Tales'* six adventures.

We are never told West's motives for wanting to perfect reanimation, but what could have started as a noble endeavor is degraded beginning in the series' first act, which is set during West's university days. West's original goal is to "restore vitality before the advent of death," but when that proves impossible[15] he switches to resuscitating the recently deceased, and, blinded by condescension towards the sanctity of life, he is soon body-snatching to get specimens for his experiments. West is horrified when one specimen goes on a cannibalistic spree, but he dismisses his own culpability by claiming the specimen was not fresh enough, however its incarceration in an insane asylum weighs upon Wests's conscience. It is never far from his thoughts. Things progress, so to speak, in the second act, set during West's days as a practioner in the blue-collar town of Bolton near Boston. When another specimen commits a singularly awful deed and brings evidence of it to West, the young doctor confronts a turning point. This time West cannot dismiss his culpability and his soul is instantly "calloused and seared," demonstrated by his threatening to bring the police to his door by shooting the specimen six times, and then by committing murder to get a fresh enough specimen to finally prove to his own satisfaction that his reagent can restore rational life. By act three there is nothing left of West's moral fiber as he succumbs to "a hellish and perverse addiction" during the First World War to create "artificial monstrosities" from the battlefield dead. West's finally goes too far, and in the process creates an arch-enemy who orchestrates his inevitable comeuppance back in Boston.

West is (surprise!, surprise!) a mad doctor, the modern archetype of which is Dr. Victor Frankenstein, and Mary Wollstonecraft Shelly's *Frankenstein, or The Modern Prometheus* (1818) is often cited as an inspiration for *Grewsome Tales* even though, as Joshi points out, "The method of West's reanimation of the dead (whole bodies that have died only recently) is very different from that of Victor Frankenstein (the assembling of a composite body from disparate parts of bodies), and only perhaps the most general influence can be detected."[16] There are other differences, the most notable being that Frankenstein never rejects that God may exist whereas West dismisses any notion of a Creator, "Holding with [Ernst] Haeckel that all life is a chemical and physical process, and the so-called *soul* is a myth[.]"[17] In this regard West has more in common with the Victor Frankenstein portrayed by Peter Cushing in Hammer Studio's Grand Guignol *Curse of Frankenstein* (1958) and its sequels. Cushing's Frankenstein is an educated man who finds everything except his quest to create life meaningless, including religion,[18] a blind spot that prevents Frankenstein from realizing he is doomed to fail because a higher moral authority controlling the universe refuses to permit him to succeed.[19] Just like in *Grewsome Tales*, the experiments of Cushing's Frankenstein degenerate from sequel to sequel, but while West is as single-minded as Cushing's Frankenstein when it comes to restoring rational life, West never completely succeeds simply because he fails, perhaps for no better reason than his theories may be wrong. Besides, what fun would there be if West did succeed? The Noble Prize would be retired in his name, he would join the pantheon of science, and we would all drink and dance and go home happy. Instead West fails and fails like Cushing's Frankenstein, until his "moral undoing" leads to him being hoisted upon his on petard.

The fact is we may never know if Shelley's *Frankenstein* was an inspiration for *Grewsome Tales*. Lovecraft never disclosed where he got the idea for the series[20] and Joshi makes a good argument that "The core of the story is so elementary a weird conception that no literary source need be postulated[.]" [21] That said, we do know Lovecraft admired *Frankenstein*, praising it at length as "inimitable" in *Supernatural Horror in Literature*,[22] and parallels exist between the stories. Victor Frankenstein is brilliant like West, but instead of Haeckel, Frankenstein becomes a disciple of natural philosophy and begins a quest for the elixir of life at age thirteen after reading some of the works of Heinrich Cornelius Agrippa. Frankenstein masters chemistry and anatomy as a college student in Ingolstadt, and while studying the cause and progress of human decay recognizes the "brilliant and wondrous, yet so simple…cause of generation and life; nay, more, I became myself capable of bestowing animation upon lifeless matter."[23] West's tumultuous relationship with Allan Halsey,[24] dean of the Miskatonic University Medical School in Arkham, Massachusetts, echoes Frankenstein's relationship with two professors of modern natural philosophy. From Frankenstein's perspective the rationalistic M. Krempe holds that scientists are "required to exchange chimeras of boundless grandeur for realities of little worth," whereas M. Waldman holds that alchemists like Agrippa may have been misguided but "whose indefatigable zeal modern philosophers were indebted for most of the foundation of their knowledge."[25] Emboldened by M. Waldman, Frankenstein redoubles his efforts and "some early discoveries in the improvement of some chemical instruments…procured me great esteem and admiration at the university."[26] In the first two *Grewsome Tales* Halsey and the professors at the medical school deny West's request to experiment on human subjects, dismissing West's theory as "nothing but the immature vagaries of a youthful enthusiast[.]" Frankenstein is more respectful to M. Krempe in public than West is to Halsey and Miskatonic's other "tradition-bound elders," and West indulges "in elaborate daydreams of revenge, triumph and final magnanimous forgiveness," but after a typhoid epidemic breaks out, West's hostility transforms into admiration as

Halsey works with patients other doctors deem past hope, and "because of this [West] was even more determined to prove to [Halsey] the truth of his amazing doctrines." Frankenstein and West become more than familiar with graveyards and body-snatching,[27] set up a laboratory/dissecting-room in secluded locations to carry out their experiments, and desert their first triumphs, abandonments which eventually lead to both doctor's destruction. West's first human subject, a "brawny young workman," sounds as physically perfect as Frankenstein imagines his Creature looks during its assemblage,[28] but where Shelley describes the Creature's birth and Frankenstein's flight in nightmarish detail,[29] the reanimation of West's first human subject occurs off-stage, the details being left to the reader's imagination, while Lovecraft injects a little of that dark humor as, in their fright, the Narrator and West scatter through a window and burn down their laboratory. In almost every adventure after this the Narrator mentions how West, worried this first subject may have escaped the fire, often fancies hearing footsteps behind him. After Frankenstein flees from his Creature, he spends the night wandering the streets, too scared to look around lest he spy his Creature pursuing him, even quoting Samuel Taylor Coleridge's 1789 poem *The Rime of the Ancient Mariner* to describe his trepidations:

> *Like one who, on a lonely road,*
> *Doth walk in fear and dread,*
> *And, having once turned round, walks on,*
> *And turns no more his head;*
> *Because he knows a frightful fiend*
> *Doth close behind him tread.*[30]

Another commonly presumed inspiration for *Grewsome Tales* is Sir Arthur Conan Doyle's Sherlock Holmes canon, which Lovecraft adored from childhood. As a boy he even organized his own detective agency.[31] Patterning serials after the most popular series in Western literature[32] was commonplace by the early 1920s, however *Supernatural Horror in Literature* demonstrates that Lovecraft was an astute enough reviewer to recognize something often overlooked when it comes to the Great Detective's success: Conan Doyle's shrewdness in tailoring Holmes to readers' needs and wants. Conan Doyle recognized before most that, if a reader missed an episode of a serial, the narrative thread would be lost, but if each installment is a complete adventure then a reader can fully devote himself to a series,[33] and while *Grewsome Tales* works as "a single entity" which "builds up a certain cumulative power and suspense,"[34] each installment does present a complete adventure in West's awesome quest. And there are other parallels. Like Dr. John H. Watson with Holmes, *Grewsome Tales'* Narrator chronicles West's adventures and is an "active and enthralled assistant," even though Lovecraft's characters do not lodge together until the series' third adventure. In the first Holmes adventure, *A Study in Scarlet* (1887), there is no dialogue and Watson's name is not mentioned until the moment he chances across an acquaintance who introduces him to Holmes, while *Grewsome Tales* features very little dialogue (which, granted, is typical in almost all of Lovecraft's stories) and we are never told the Narrator's name. Like Holmes, we are introduced to West in a medical setting (Holmes at St. Bartholomew's Hospital and West at Miskatonic University Medical School) and never learn much about the protagonist's past. Holmes and West are both brilliant but dispassionate men convinced of the overwhelming importance of their work, and echoes of Watson's famous admonition of Holmes from their second adventure, the 1890 novel *The Sign of Four* ("You really are an automaton—a calculating machine…there is something positively inhuman about you at times.")[35] can be heard in the second West adventure where the Narrator describes how West's unassuming visage "gave no hint of the supernormal—almost diabolical—power of the cold brain within."[36] Lovecraft even gives West a Moriarty figure in Sir Eric Moreland Clapham-Lee.

Possible inspirations aside, *Grewsome Tales* is "universally acknowledged as Lovecraft's poorest work,"[37] but this is no reason to dismiss the series or assume it is dreadful. Let us imagine that Lovecraft had submitted *Grewsome Tales* to a creative writing class instead of writing it for *Home Brew*. How would an instructor rate it?

The plot structure is formulaic, which is understandable in a serial. The plot structure is just as formulaic in "The Lurking Fear," but formula plots are atypical in Lovecraft's earlier and contemporaneous fiction, which range from relatively conventional to very good in their own right,[38] plus *Grewsome Tales'* plot construction and West's moral degradation demonstrate "some skill" as it "builds in neat, logical increments from one section to the next[.]"[39]

The characters are at time inexcusably cliché, several are stereotypes, and Lovecraft often tells us rather than shows us what they do. This last point is not really a problem when the Narrator describes activities he and West participate in, but supporting characters suffer, none more than Halsey in "The Plague-Daemon." Telling the reader about Halsey's selfless dedication battling a typhoid epidemic makes us admire the dean, but presenting specifics about how Halsey refused to abandon patients until he worked himself to death could have elicited sympathy, which would make what happens next to Halsey and to Arkham more shocking and heartbreaking. Instead, Lovecraft makes the rookie mistake of wasting words earlier in the story to overemphasize Halsey's and the professors' closed-minded nature that could have been put to better use here.

As previously mentioned, each adventure's word count handicapped Lovecraft when it comes to cultivating the sort of atmosphere he believed is paramount to a horror story's success. Nevertheless, all six *Grewsome Tales* do lead up to a weird denouement in the final episode, and if Lovecraft's intent was to create an unsettling atmosphere in the series' conclusion he was not unsuccessful. At the same time many events in *Grewsome Tales* are not merely gruesome but sensational, and Lovecraft makes the most of a number of them by suggesting rather than reciting what happens, such as the first reanimation. While Lovecraft is occasionally prone to overwriting and hyperbole -- the opening paragraph of "The Plague-Daemon" is a good example -- he just as frequently does an excellent job of driving home specific moments of horror in a sentence or two. Examples of this include an apparent attempt by someone to dig up a new grave in Arkham's potter's field by hand in "From the Dark" and West and the Narrator "making a night of it" with a corpse in "The Plague-Daemon."

Overall this is a C+ effort that has enough bright spots to suggest its author will soon be creating better things. However, this general assessment does an injustice to the third adventure "Six Shots by Moonlight," a standout B+ effort that demonstrates Lovecraft's potential in action. While this story suffers as much as its companions from clichés and stereotypes, here Lovecraft manipulates Houtain's word count to his advantage. Rather than merely recapping highlights from West's previous two stories, Lovecraft mixes adequate background information about West, the Narrator, and their goals with an introduction of their new home in Bolton while creating some Gothic atmosphere in an opening that is as good as the preamble to most of Lovecraft's other contemporaneous stories. The reader is drawn into this adventure rather than drug through it, and if the conclusion has a whiff of W.W. Jacobs' "The Monkey's Paw" (1902), unlike that "able melodramatic bit"[40] Lovecraft throws open the door at the end to show the monster knocking on the other side to present a snapshot of a grotesquerie that may be expected but is still chilling enough to devastate West's soul. This is a lurid story, but not as lurid as its companions, relying less on Grand Guignol and more on measured suspense to create a tragic terror. "Six Shots by Moonlight" stands on its own as a better than average example of pulp magazine horror.

* * *

Lovecraft died in Providence on March 15, 1937, and with a few exceptions, such as Dashiell Hammett's *Creeps by Night* (1931), an anthology of magazine horror fiction[41] that included "The Music of Erich Zann" (1921), the gentleman author from Rhode Island died unnoticed by his era's mainstream media. If not for the efforts of August Derleth and Donald Wandrei at Arkham House to keep Lovecraft's weird stories in print, it is possible they might have slipped into total obscurity. But even though none of Lovecraft's fiction was adapted for radio or motion picture during his lifetime, *Grewsome Tales* appears to be one of many influences running rampant in *Maniac* (1934), an exploitation film that foreshadows some of the impudence, violence, and nudity of *Re-Animator*.

Mad scientist Dr. Meirschultz (Horace Carpenter) is working on a reagent to reanimate the dead and has gone as far as he can experimenting on animal subjects. Meirschultz and his assistant Don Maxwell (Bill Woods) finagle their way into a marvelous Gothic-looking morgue, where they try the reagent on a human subject and reanimate Maria Altura,[42] a beautiful young woman who killed herself using carbon monoxide. Although Altura's resuscitated condition is somnambulistic, Meirschultz is satisfied enough to take his research to the next level by transplanting a heart he is keeping alive into a dead body, which he wants Maxwell to provide by committing suicide. At this point *Grewsome Tales'* influence dissipates as the movie grows more twisted while several actresses seem to have increasing difficulty keeping on their clothes.

Between *Maniac* and *Re-Animator* came another film possibly influenced by *Grewsome Tales*, one of Universal Studio's horror classics, *The Mad Ghoul*, which was released in 1943, one year after *Grewsome Tales* was reprinted as *Herbert West: Reanimator* in the long-running pulp magazine *Weird Tales*.

In this undervalued film mad doctor Alfred Morris (George Zucco), a chemistry professor, has a horrible gas used by the Mayans during possible religious rights. The gas kills by putting its victims into a "state of life in death" where these ghouls can be controlled before being temporarily restored to life using a substance from the human heart. Morris wants to discover a way to permanently reverse the killing action of the gas, and recruits surgical student Ted Allison (David Bruce) to assist with his research during summer break. Morris is also carrying a torch for Ted's girlfriend Isabel Lewis (Evelyn Akers), a concert singer preparing to go on a tour that could establish her career. One night Isabel confides to Morris that she no longer loves Ted. Isabel loves someone else, and the professor deludes himself into thinking she has fallen for him, even though he is old enough to be her father. This is bad news for Ted, because when it comes to notions of right and wrong Morris is in lockstep with Cushing's Frankenstein and Combs' West. Earlier in the film Morris even tells Ted, "I'm a scientist. To me there is no good or evil, only true or false. Work with one; discard the other." Morris turns the gas on an unsuspecting Ted so the professor can command him to break up with Isabel. To give Morris his due, he is confidant he will discover how to reverse the gas' action and permanently restore Ted to a normal life, but these plans are put on the back burner after Morris discovers Isabel actually loves her pianist Eric Iverson (Turhan Bey). Morris waits for Ted to relapse into a ghoul state, then orders Ted to kill Eric, thus clearing the way for Isabel to fall in love with Morris; but something always gets in the way, so Morris follows Isabel's tour with Ted, digging up a body or murdering someone at each stop to get more heart substance to keep Ted "alive" and in the professor's control. Eventually Ted figures out what Morris is doing and turns the table by exposing Morris to the gas before succumbing to another relapse. Ted is gunned down making one last attempt to kill Eric, and the last time we see Morris he is futilely clawing his way into a grave to get at the corpse's heart before succumbing to the gas' death state.

The Mad Ghoul could have been a lackluster B-movie with only an unusually gruesome plot to set it apart from other horror films, but like *Re-Animator* it features a wonderful cast, fine direction, and a clever script that mixes original and traditional horror with gallows humor.[43] A good example takes place in one of the film's best and most ghastly scenes. Ken McClure (Robert Armstrong), a hardnosed reporter from the Ben Hecht and Carl Kolchak School of Journalism, lays a trap for the "ghoul" killer in a mortuary by pretending to be a corpse in a coffin. When Morris arrives McClure aims a gun at the professor, who drolls, "Reports of your death seem to be greatly exaggerated." Ted creeps up on McClure, who is still in the coffin, and distracts the reporter, who drops his gun. Morris strangles McClure and then waits for Ted to cut out the reporter's heart. Morris is just as driven in his scientific pursuits as West, and he is just as merciless in his pursuit of a younger woman as *Re-Animator's* Dr. Carl Hill (David Gale), West's arch-enemy who is in love with Megan Halsey (Barbara Crampton).[44] Morris, like West, suffers no qualms about manipulating other people to get what he wants, and both films feature college campuses and pivotal scenes in a cemetery, mortuary, or morgue that involve the mutilation of the dead.

Grewsome Tales was finally albeit briefly adapted by EC Comics in 1950,[45] but except for being a possible influence for Dr. Anton Arcane and his synthetic Un-Men from DC Comics' landmark 1970s horror-adventure series *Swamp Thing*,[46] Herbert West drifted into anonymity until the 1985 release of *Re-Animator*.

The idea of adapting West's adventures into a movie started with Stuart Gordon, a film and horror fan best known at the time as a stage director, art director, playwright, and founder of Chicago's Organic Theater. Gordon's theatrical credits at the time included *Warp!* and *E/R Emergency Room*, the latter turned into a short-lived television program (1984-5) starring Elliot Gould. Gordon tried and failed to pitch *Re-Animator* as a television series after being urged to come to Hollywood by special effects man Bob Greenberg, who was convinced that *Re-Animator* should be a movie. To that end

Greenburg introduced Gordon to a young producer named Brian Yuzna, who agreed with Greenburg but only if Gordon pulled out all the stops.[47]

The rest, as they say, is history.

More impudent than *Maniac* and an even more nimble combination of original and traditional horror than *The Mad Ghoul*, *Re-Animator* was hailed as a welcome change of pace to film critics and horror fans tired of slasher films.[48] Since the film's release the image of Combs' bespectacled West wielding a syringe of glowing anti-freeze green reanimation fluid has become almost as iconic as Michael Meyers in his green coveralls, Freddy Krueger flashing his razor-tipped glove, and Jason Voorhees in his hockey mask, and the movie was popular enough to spawn two sequels (along with serious discussions about a third Herbert West film and a television series), a successful musical written and directed by Gordon, and several comic books starting with a 1991 adaptation form Malibu Graphics.

Which brings us to some annoyingly autobiographical but hopefully interesting behind-the-scenes information.

Malibu Graphics was one of the most successful independent comics publishers of the Eighties and Nineties, and in 1990 signed a licensing deal with Full Moon Productions to publish comics based on some of the studio's films. I found out about this when I called Malibu's creative director Tom Mason to inquire if a rumor was true and the company was launching a new series based on the *Planet of the Apes* franchise. The rumor was true, but another writer was already assigned to that series, but then Tom asked me if I had ever heard of a Full Moon film called *Re-Animator*.

Honestly, I thought he was kidding.

Tom is not a fan of gory horror films, so he knew nothing about *Re-Animator* or its cult film status. I brought him up to speed and Tom kindly offered me first crack at writing an adaptation of the movie. Three synopses and a proposal later the gig was mine. I then asked Tom if Christopher Jones (*Young Justice, Batman '66*) could draw the book. Christopher and I broke into comics in 1987 on the series *Street Heroes 2005* and I knew he would do a fabulous job on this adaptation. A few pieces of sample artwork later Christopher was on board, too. I must have been on quite a roll because I also convinced Malibu into letting me edit the first mass-market anthology of Lovecraft's original *Grewsome Tales* in conjunction with the comics adaptation. That anthology sold well but has been long out of print, although copies can still be purchased on Amazon and eBay under the title *Re-Animator: Tales of Herbert West*. As for the *Re-Animator* adaptation, it was successful enough to merit an original prequel,[49] one Christopher and I were not involved with, although we did team up again a few years later to adapt Lovecraft's short story "The Statement of Randolph Carter" for Caliber Comics' *Worlds of H. P. Lovecraft*.

* * *

Which brings us to this new edition of Lovecraft's *Grewsome Tales* accompanied with *Supernatural Horror in Literature*.

Thanks to *Re-Animator* the original Herbert West adventures are no longer obscure. Since the film's release the series has been reprinted in numerous Lovecraft and horror anthologies and can be found on the Internet along with audio versions including one read by Combs. Also thanks to the film's popularity, I have had the opportunity to adapt several of Lovecraft's other short stories like "The Statement of Randolph Carter" into comics for Malibu, Caliber Comics, and Transfuzion Publishing. These comics adaptations have been available in print or in digital since their first publications, but I never thought about reprinting the series' anthology until a reviewer named Matthew T. Carpenter suggested it on my Amazon author's page.

I liked the idea, but a new edition should at least offer some new material, so I contacted Justin Beahm, the author of several excellent articles on horror films as well as a rising star in the horror film community, who agreed to contribute the foreword, while Caliber's publisher h solicited new illustrations. For several years I have wanted to produce an audio adaptation of "From the Dark," and my script appears here for the first time. I have also often wondered just what the heck happened to West after *Grewsome Tales*. If there was ever a character who would not go quietly into that good night it is Herbert West, so I present my own suggestions about that in a new adventure written for this anthology. Finally, since I make several references to *Supernatural Horror in Literature* in this introduction, I thought it would be useful and instructive to include Lovecraft's important essay on horror literature as well, and I am grateful to S. T. Joshi for contributing the corrected text for this anthology, and Lovecraft Holdings LLC for granting permission to reprint it here.

And so here we are, almost one hundred years since the publication of *Grewsome Tales* in *Home Brew* and thirty years since the release of *Re-Animator*. During that time Herbert West has experienced the same renaissance as his creator, going from being nearly forgotten to becoming a horror icon. Besides being Lovecraft's most traditional horror creation, West is Lovecraft's best known creation after Cthuhlu. Who can say what fate awaits West over the next century?

Steven Philip Jones
Cedar Rapids/Iowa City: April 2015

Endnotes

---

[1] In *A Dreamer and a Visionary: H. P. Lovecraft in His Time*, S. T. Joshi cites the cause of death for Winfield Scott as "general paresis" and adds, "Although general paresis was a kind of catch-all term for a variety of ailments, M. Eileen McNamara, M.D., studying Winfield's medical record, has concluded that the probability of Winfield's having tertiary syphilis is very strong…It is difficult to doubt that Winfield contracted syphilis either from a prostitute or from some other sex partner prior to his marriage, either while attending the military academy or during his stint as a 'Commercial Traveler,' if indeed that began so early as the age of twenty-eight (pp. 13-4)."
[2] *H. P. Lovecraft*, pp. 2-3
[3] Houtain reportedly instructed that Lovecraft could not make these stories too morbid (*A Dreamer and a Visionary*, p. 151).
[4] http://www.philsp.com/data/data184.html
[5] Houtain commissioned a second Lovecraft series, "The Lurking Fear," and published it in its entirety before *Home Brew* went out of business in April 1923. The magazine continued under a different name, *High Life*, until May 1924.

[6] Some might argue that Lovecraft's alter ego Randolph Carter is a series character, but Carter appears in a handful of stories mostly set in Lovecraft's dream-world that were written over a period of years and not at all conceived as a series like *Grewsome Tales*.

[7] Lovecraft describes this as being ordered to "drag one character through a series of artificial episodes (*Call of Cthulhu and Other Weird Stories*, p. 375)."

[8] Stuart Gordon, director and co-screenwriter of *Re-Animator*, points out that Lovecraft's stories do feature "little gags…but it is definitely true there [are] very few knee-slappers in an H. P. Lovecraft story (*Horror Film Directors*, p. 490)."

[9] Lovecraft also spent some of those words recapping the previous episode, but Joshi makes a good point that Lovecraft could have gotten around this problem by having Houtain include headnotes before each episode. "Lovecraft learned better in his second *Home Brew* serial, 'The Lurking Fear,' where he must have instructed Houtain to provide just such synopses to free him from the burden of doing so (*Call of Cthulhu and Other Weird Stories*, p. 375)."

[10] "Atmosphere is the all-important thing, for the final criterion of authenticity is not the dovetailing of a plot but the creation of a given sensation (see *Supernatural Horror in Literature*)."

[11] Compare any *Grewsome Tales* episode to the first paragraph of one of Lovecraft's best stories, "The Colour Out of Space," to see what I mean.

[12] Gordon claims that one of the reasons he was drawn to Lovecraft's Hebert West tales "was that I felt it was, for Lovecraft, a very explicit story (*Horror Film Directors*, p. 490)."

[13] *Call of Cthulhu and Other Weird Stories*, p. 375

[14] Ibid

[15] Perhaps these failures earned Death the same hostility from West that West nurtures for Dean Allan Halsey for rejecting his theory, but such vindictiveness almost pales when compared to the hubris of Mary Wollstonecraft Shelley's Victor Frankenstein. It is understandable that a thirteen-year-old Frankenstein might fantasize about the "glory [that] would attend the discovery if I could banish disease from the human frame and render man invulnerable to any but a violent death (*Frankenstein*, p. 29)!" Frankenstein is an university student, however, when he contemplates that "Life and death appeared to me ideal bounds, which I should first break through and pour a torrent of light into our dark world. A new species would bless me as its creator and source; many happy and excellent natures would owe their being to me. No father could claim the gratitude of his child so completely as I should deserve theirs (ibid, p. 41)."

[16] *Call of Cthulhu and Other Weird Stories*, p. 375. Joshi fails to point out that eventually West does work with individual body parts, although West has no interest in assembling them into one whole person, while Frankenstein expresses interest in something like reanimation: "Pursing these reflections, I thought that if I could bestow animation upon lifeless matter, I might in the process of time (although I now found it impossible) renew life where death had apparently devoted the body to corruption (*Frankenstein*, p. 41)." Once again, freshness seems to be a problem, although it begs the question why Frankenstein does not have this problem with body parts assembled into a whole body.

[17] See *Call of Cthulhu and Other Weird Stories*, p. 376 and Peter Canon's *H. P. Lovecraft*, p. 40.

[18] In a stunning example of spiritual myopia, Cushing's Frankenstein manages to ignore the possibility of something greater than Man even after discovering a means of transferring the soul in *Frankenstein Created Woman* (1967), which brings new meaning to the phrase "blinded by ambition."

[19] From *Terence Fisher* by Paul Legget: "[In the Hammer films Victor] Frankenstein is a rebel in a world ultimately ruled by God. Frankenstein inevitably fails because he is limited by a spiritual and moral authority which ultimately frustrates him even without his knowing it. Conversely, the psychotic killers from *Horrors of the Black Museum* to *The Silence of the Lambs* inhabit a spiritually vacuous world in which chaos predominates. These films portray a violent world of spiritual desperation which is all too clearly seen in the evening news. Fisher would agree with these films to a point. He never accepted a spiritually empty world. However, he would argue that to attempt to live apart form God is to live in chaos. The image of the psychotic killer symbolizes a world turned away from God in which there is no restraint. This is hardly a 'modern' or even 'post-modern' view. The fearful consequences of seeking to live apart from any divine restraint are portrayed again and again in the Bible (pp. 187-8)."

[20] The Wikipedia entry for *Herbert West-Reanimator* claims Lovecraft writes in his letters that the story is a parody of *Frankenstein* but fails to cite which letters (http://en.wikipedia.org/wiki/Herbert_West%E2%80%93Reanimator).

[21] *Call of Cthulhu and Other Weird Stories*, p. 375

[22] See *Supernatural Horror in Literature*.

[23] *Frankenstein, or The Modern Prometheus*, p. 39

[24] Like *Frankenstein* Lovecraft praises Edgar Allan Poe in *Supernatural Horror in Literature*, devoting an entire chapter to him, and Poe was one of Lovecraft's strongest influences as a writer. So is it possible the double l's in Dean Halsey's first name is a tip-of-the-hat to Poe? And while we are on the subject of names, might West's last name be an ironic comment on the American impulse to seek out new discoveries and expand the human condition, best typified by the western expansion of the 19th Century? West, like Frankenstein and many of Lovecraft's future protagonists, discover that there are some things Man is not meant to know.

[25] *Frankenstein*, pp. 35 & 37

[26] Ibid, pp. 38-9

[27] These locales and activities provide some of the most gripping moments in *Grewsome Tales* and *Frankenstein*. For example, compare West and the Narrator's exhumation of the drowned workman in "From the Dark" to this account by Frankenstein: "Who shall conceive the horrors of my secret toil as I dabbled among the unhallowed damps of the grave…I collected bones from charnel houses and disturbed, with profane fingers, the tremendous secrets of the human frame (*Frankenstein*, p. 42)."

[28] "His limbs were in proportion, and I had selected his features as beautiful (ibid, p. 45)."

[29] Lovecraft writes, "Some of the scenes in *Frankenstein* are unforgettable, as when the newly animated monster enters its creator's room, parts the curtains of his bed, and gazes at him in the yellow moonlight with watery eyes – 'if eyes they may be called (see *Supernatural Horror in Literature*.'"

[30] *Frankenstein*, p. 46

[31] See *H. P. Lovecraft*, pp. 2-3.

[32] As pulp magazine historian Robert Sampson writes, "[Holmes] was a fascinating, sharply realized, and virulently influential figure. Like a huge sun, Holmes warmed generations of imitators (*Yesterday's Faces: Vol. IV, The Solvers*, p. 3)."

[33] See *The Doctor and the Detective*, p. 141.

[34] See *A Dreamer and a Visionary*, pp 151.

[35] *The Annotated Sherlock Holmes*, p. 619

[36] Ironically, at least in a series about reanimating the dead, West appears to age very little over the years.

---

[37] *The Scriptorium: "H. P. Lovecraft,"*
http://www.themodernword.com/scriptorium/lovecraft.html
[38] See *A Dreamer and a Visionary,* pp 108 & 139.
[39] *H. P. Lovecraft*, p. 39
[40] See *Supernatural Horror in Literature.*
[41] Joshi ranks *Creeps by Night* as "one of the most heterogeneous weird-anthologies ever compiled, containing everything from the cosmic horror of Donald Wandrei's 'The Red Brain' to John Collier's *conte cruel*, 'Green Thoughts' ("Introduction," *Supernatural Horror in Literature*, p. 21)."
[42] The actress who portrays Maria Altura is not identified in the film's credits.
[43] The authors of *Universal Horrors: The Studio's Classic Films, 1931-1946,* Tom Weaver, Michael Brunas, and John Brunas, write, "There's no shortage of carnage, either visualized or implied, in *The Mad Ghoul*, yet the film manages to stay within the guidelines of accepted standards for the period it was made…*The Mad Ghoul* is several cuts above the average grindhouse quickie released by the likes of Columbia, Monogram and PRC (pp. 390 & 392)." *The Mad Ghoul* also boasts one of the finest monster make-ups by Jack Pierce, the man responsible for iconic creations like Karloff's Frankenstein Monster and Lon Chaney Jr.'s Wolf Man. Despite its lack of physical mutilation, Pierce's make-up for Ted as a mind-controlled ghoul is a remarkable precursor of contemporary zombie make-up.
[44] I doubt the authors of *Universal Horror* would feel any more sympathy for Hill than they do Morris, who they describe as "a cockeye optimist with lascivious designs on a woman young enough to be his daughter (p. 387)," but speaking as a middle aged man I would like to point out that…my gosh, we are talking about Evelyn Akers here. I do not condone his actions, but there is no denying Morris has good taste.
[45] See "Experiment in…Death!" in *Weird Science #12* (May 1950).
[46] *Swamp Thing* was created by writer Len Wein, perhaps best known today for creating Marvel Comics' Wolverine, and noted horror artist Berni Wrightson (*Frankenstein, Creepshow*). Arcane is a mad scientist and magician obsessed with immortality, and his heterogeneous artificial monstrosities the Un-Men are the results of his experiments upon the dead. Unlike the heterogeneous abominations created by West, the Un-Men are fanatically devoted to their creator. Arcane and the Un-Men first appeared in *Swamp Thing* #2 "The Man Who Wanted Forever" and returned in Swamp Thing #10 "The Man Who Would Not Die."
[47] *Horror Film Directors*, pp. 483-5
[48] This is not to suggest that the 1980s was nothing but a wasteland of slaughter films. These films just seemed to saturate the horror market, but along with *Re-Animator* there were some excellent horror films in the classic tradition such as *An American Werewolf in London* (1981), *The Fog*, (1980), and *The Dead Zone* (1983) to name a few.
[49] Our adaptation's first issue also sported a gorgeous cover of West holding up Hill's head by Dave Dorman (*Star Wars*) that Malibu simultaneously released as a poster, and since then Dorman's cover art has appeared on other *Re-Animator* licensed properties. The adaptation also features several in-jokes, starting with Kato from *The Green Hornet* picking West up at the airport on page one. (Christopher was trying out for a *Green Hornet* mini-series at the time.) The license plate number on Kato's limousine should also be familiar to any *Star Trek* fans. (I like to think that this is an indication that Kato may be one of Mr. Sulu's ancestors.) Hill's lecture hall is in the Samuel B. Mumford Hall, named after the Samuel B. Mumford House, Lovecraft's last residence before his death. Lovecraft featured this house in "The Haunter in the Dark" and Christopher and I featured it in *Re-Animator* (minus its second floor) as the house Daniel Cain (Bruce Abbott) and West live in, which

sits on the corner of Pickman ("Pickman's Model") and Peabody (from a Lovecraftian *Night Gallery* episode called "Professor Peabody's Last Lecture"). An Elway poster in Cain's house is a reference to John Elway, who quarterbacked my favorite NFL team the Denver Broncos to two Super Bowl victories, and a letterman jacket Cain wears is from my alma mater the University of Iowa. Finally an Amana refrigerator in West's bedroom where he keeps his reanimator fluid is a tip of the hat to the world-famous Amana appliance factory a few miles from where I live in eastern Iowa.

Grewsome Tales

"…all life is a chemical and physical process, and the so-called soul is a myth…"

FROM THE DARK

Of Herbert West, who was my friend in college, and in after life, I can speak only with extreme terror. This terror is not due altogether to the sinister manner of his recent disappearance, but was engendered by the whole nature of his lifework, years ago, when we were in the third year of our course at the Miskatonic University Medical School in Arkham. While he was with me, the wonder and diabolism of his experiments fascinated me utterly, and I was his closest companion. Now that he is gone and the spell is broken, the actual fear is greater. Memories and possibilities are ever more hideous than realities.

* * *

The first horrible incident of our acquaintance was the greatest shock I ever experienced, and it is only with reluctance I repeat it. As I have said, it happened when were in medical school, where West had already made himself notorious through his wild theories on the nature of death and the possibility of overcoming it artificially. His views, which were widely ridiculed by the faculty and by his fellow students, hinged on the essentially mechanistic nature of life; and concerned means of operating the organic machinery of mankind by calculated chemical action after the failure of natural processes. In his experiments with various animating solutions he had killed and treated immense numbers of rabbits, guinea-pigs, cats, dogs and monkeys, till he had become the prime nuisance of the college. Several times he had actually obtained signs of life in the animals supposedly dead; in many cases violent signs; but he soon saw that the perfection of his process, if indeed possible, would necessarily involved a lifetime of research. It likewise became clear that, since the same solution never worked alike on different organic species, he would require human subjects for further and more specialised progress. It was here he first came into conflict with the college authorities, and was debarred from future experiments by no less a dignitary than the dean of the medical school himself—the learned and benevolent Dr. Allan Halsey, whose work in behalf of the stricken is recalled by every old resident of Arkham.

I had always been exceptionally tolerant of West's pursuits, and we frequently discussed his theories, whose ramifications and corollaries were almost infinite. Holding with Haeckel that all life is a chemical and physical process, and the so-called soul is a myth, my friend believed artificial reanimation of the dead can depend only on the condition of the tissues; and unless actual decomposition has set in, a corpse fully equipped with organs may with suitable measures be set going again in the peculiar fashion known as life. That the psychic or intellectual life might be impaired by the slight deterioration of sensitive brain cells which even a short period of death would be apt to cause, West fully realised. It had first been his hope to find a reagent which would restore vitality before the actual advent of death, and only repeated failures on animals had shewn him the natural and artificial life-motions were incompatible. He then sought extreme freshness in his specimens, injecting his solutions into the blood immediately after the extinction of life. It was this circumstance which made the professors so carelessly skeptical, for they felt true death had not occurred in any case. They did not stop to view the matter closely and reasonably.

* * *

It was not long after the faculty had interdicted his work that West confided to me his resolution to get fresh human bodies in some manner, and continue in secret the experiments he could no longer perform openly. To hear him discussing ways and means was rather ghastly, for at the college we had never procured anatomical specimens ourselves. Whenever the morgue proved inadequate, two local Negroes attended to this matter, and they were seldom questioned. West was then a small, slender, spectacled youth with delicate features, yellow hair, pale blue eyes and a soft voice, and it was uncanny to hear him dwelling on the relative merits of Christchurch Cemetery and the potter's field, because practically everybody in Christchurch was embalmed; a thing of course ruinous to West's researches.

I was by this time his active and enthralled assistant, and helped him make all his decisions, not only concerning the source of bodies but a suitable place for our loathsome work. It was I who thought of the deserted Chapman farmhouse beyond Meadow Hill, where we fitted up on the ground floor an operating room and a laboratory, each with dark curtains to conceal our midnight doings. The place was far from any road, and in sight of no other house, yet precautions were none the less necessary; since rumours of strange lights, started by chance nocturnal roamers, would soon bring disaster on our enterprise. It was agreed to call the whole thing a chemical laboratory if discovery should occur. Gradually we equipped our sinister haunt of science with materials either purchased in Boston or quietly borrowed from the college—materials carefully made unrecognisable save to expert eyes—and provided spades and picks for the many burials we should have to make in the cellar. At the college we used an incinerator, but the apparatus was too costly for our unauthorised laboratory. Bodies were always a nuisance—even the small guinea-pig bodies from the slight clandestine experiments in West's room at the boarding-house.

We followed the local death-notices like ghouls, for our specimens demanded particular qualities. What we wanted were corpses interred soon after death and without artificial preservation, preferably free from malforming disease, and certainly with all organs present. Accident victims were our best hope. Not for many weeks did we hear of anything suitable; though we talked with morgue and hospital authorities, ostensibly in the college's interest, as often as we could without exciting suspicion. We found the college had first choice in every case, so that it might be necessary to remain in Arkham during the summer, when only the limited summer-school classes were held. In the end, though, luck favoured us; for one day we heard of an almost ideal case in the potter's field: a brawny young workman drowned only the morning before in Sumner's Pond, and buried at the town's expense without delay or embalming. That afternoon we found the new grave, and determined to begin work soon after midnight.

* * *

It was a repulsive task we undertook in the black small hours, even though we lacked at that time the special horror of graveyards which later experiences brought to us. We carried spades and oil dark lanterns, for although electric torches were then manufactured, they were not as satisfactory as the tungsten contrivances of today. The process of unearthing was slow and sordid—it might have been gruesomely poetical if we had been artists instead of scientists—and we were glad when our spades struck wood. When the pine box was fully uncovered West scrambled down and removed the lid, dragging out and propping up the contents. I reached down and hauled the contents out of the grave, and then both toiled hard to restore the spot to its former appearance. The affair made us rather nervous, especially the stiff form and vacant face of our first trophy, but we managed to remove all traces of our visit. When we had patted down the last shovelful of earth we put the specimen in a canvas sack and set out for the old Chapman place beyond Meadow Hill.

On an improvised dissecting-table in the old farmhouse, by the light of a powerful acetylene lamp, the specimen was not very spectral looking. It had been a sturdy and apparently unimaginative youth of wholesome plebian type—large-framed, grey-eyed and brown-haired—a sound animal without psychological subtleties, and probably having vital processes of the simplest and healthiest sort. Now, with the eyes closed, it looked more asleep than dead; though the expert test of my friend soon left no doubt on that score. We had at last what West had always longed for: a real dead man of the ideal kind, ready for the solution as prepared according to the most careful calculations and theories for human use. The tension on our part became very great. We knew there was scarcely a chance for anything like complete success, and could not avoid hideous fears at possible grotesque results of partial animation. Especially were we appreciative concerning the mind and impulses of the creature, since in the space following death some of the more delicate cerebral cells might well have suffered deterioration. I, myself, still held some curious notions about the traditional *soul* of man, and felt an awe at the secrets that might be told by one returning from the dead. I wondered what sights this placid youth might have seen in inaccessible spheres, and what he could relate if fully restored to life. But my wonder was not overwhelming, since for the most part I shared the materialism of my friend. He was calmer than I as he forced a large quantity of his fluid into a vein of the body's arm, immediately binding the incision securely.

The waiting was gruesome, but West never faltered. Every now and then he applied his stethoscope to the specimen, and bore the negative results philosophically. After about three-quarters of an hour without the least sign of life he disappointingly pronounced the solution inadequate, but determined to make the most of his opportunity and try one change in the formula before disposing of his ghastly prize. We had that afternoon dug a grave in the cellar, and would have to fill it by dawn—for although we had fixed a lock on the house we wished to shun even the remotest risk of a ghoulish discovery. Besides, the body would not be even approximately fresh the next night. So taking the solitary acetylene lamp into the adjacent laboratory, we left our silent guest on the slab in the dark, and bent every energy to the mixing of a new solution, the weighing and measuring supervised by West an almost fanatical care.

The awful event was very sudden and wholly unexpected. I was pouring something from one test-tube to another, and West was busy over the alcohol blast-lamp which had to answer for a Bunsen burner in this gasless edifice, when from the pitch-black room we had left there burst the most appalling and daemonic succession of cries either of us had ever heard. Not more unutterable could have been the chaos of hellish sound if the pit itself had opened to release the agony of the damned, for in one inconceivable cacophony was centered all the supernal terror and unnatural despair of animate nature. Human it could not have been – it is not in man to make such sounds—and without a thought of our late employment or its possible discovery both West and I leapt to the nearest window like stricken animals; overturning tubes, lamps and retorts, and vaulting madly into the starred abyss of the rural night. I think we screamed ourselves as we stumbled frantically toward the town, though as we reached the outskirts we put on a semblance of restraint—just enough to seem like belated revelers staggering home from a debauch.

* * *

We did not separate, but managed to get to West's room, where we whispered with the gas up until dawn. By then we had calmed ourselves a little with rational theories and plans for investigation, so that we could sleep through the day, classes being disregarded. But that evening two items in the paper, wholly unrelated, made it again impossible for us to sleep. The old deserted Chapman house had inexplicably burned to an amorphous heap of ashes; that we could understand because of the upset lamp. Also, an attempt had been made to disturb a new grave in the potter's field, as if by futile and spadeless clawing at the earth. That we could not understand, for we had patted down the mould very carefully.

And for seventeen years after that West would look frequently over his shoulder, and complain of fancied footsteps behind him. Now he has disappeared.

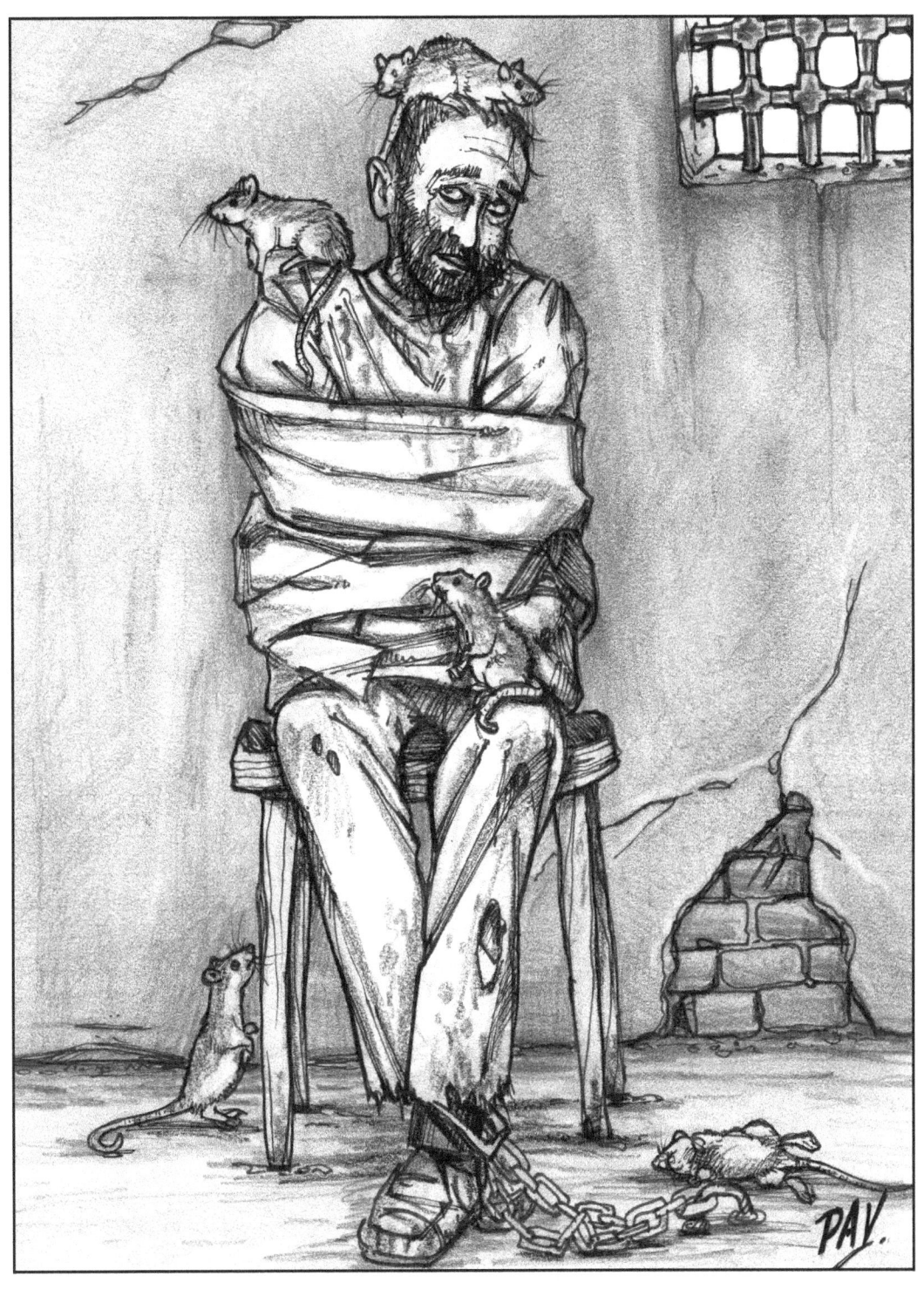

"…so many fresh specimens, yet none for his persecuted researches!"

THE PLAGUE-DAEMON

I shall never forget that hideous summer sixteen years ago, when like a noxious afreet from the halls of Eblis typhoid stalked leeringly through Arkham. It is by that satanic scourge most recall the year, for truly terror brooded with bat-wings over the piles of coffins in the tombs of Christchurch Cemetery; yet for me there is a greater horror in that time—a horror known to me alone now that Herbert West has disappeared.

* * *

West and I were doing post-graduate work in summer classes at the medical school of Miskatonic University, and my friend had attained a wide notoriety because of his experiments leading toward the revivification of the dead. After the scientific slaughter of uncounted small animals the freakish work had ostensibly stopped by order of our sceptical dean, Dr. Allan Halsey; though West had continued to perform certain secret tests in his dingy boarding-house room, and on one terrible and unforgettable occasion taken a human body from its grave in the potter's field to a deserted farm beyond Meadow Hill.

I was with him on that odious occasion, and saw him inject into the still veins the elixir which he thought would to some extent restore life's chemical and physical processes. It had ended horribly—in a delirium of fear which we gradually came to attribute to our own overwrought nerves—and West had never afterward been able to shake off a maddening sensation of being haunted and hunted. The body had not been quite fresh enough; it is obvious to restore normal mental attributes a body must be very fresh indeed; and the burning of the old house had prevented us from burying the thing. It would have been better if we could have known it was underground.

After that experience West dropped his researches for some time; but as the zeal of the born scientist slowly returned, he again became importunate with the college faculty, pleading for the use of the dissecting-room and of fresh human specimens for the work he regarded as so overwhelmingly important. His pleas, however, were wholly in vain, for the decision of Dean Halsey was inflexible, and the other professors all endorsed the verdict of their leader. In the radical theory of reanimation they saw nothing but the immature vagaries of a youthful enthusiast whose slight form, yellow hair, spectacled blue eyes and soft voice gave no hint of the supernormal—almost diabolical—power of the cold brain within. I can see him now as he was then, and I shiver. He grew sterner of face, but never elderly. And now Sefton Asylum has had the mishap and West has vanished.

West clashed disagreeably with Dr. Halsey near the end of our last undergraduate term in a wordy dispute that did less credit to him than to the kindly dean in point of courtesy. He felt he was being needlessly and irrationally retarded in a supremely great work; a work which he could of course conduct to suit himself in later years, but which he wished to begin while still possessed of the exceptional facilities of the university. That the tradition-bound elders should ignore his singular results on animals, and persist in their denial of the possibility of reanimation, was inexpressibly disgusting and almost incomprehensible to a youth of West's logical temperament. Only greater maturity could help him understand the chronic mental limitations of the *professor-doctor* type, the product of generations of pathetic Puritanism: kindly, conscientious and sometimes gentle and amiable, yet always narrow, intolerant, custom-ridden and lacking in perspective. Age has more charity for these incomplete yet high-souled characters, whose worst real vice is timidity, and who are ultimately punished by general ridicule for their intellectual sins—sins like Ptolemaism, Calvinism, anti-Darwinism, anti-Nietzscheanism, and every sort of Sabbatarianism and sumptuary legislation. West, young despite his marvelous scientific acquirements, had scant patience with good Dr. Halsey and his erudite colleagues, and nursed an increasing resentment, coupled with a desire to prove his theories to these obtuse worthies in some striking and dramatic fashion. Like most youths, he indulged in elaborate daydreams of revenge, triumph and final magnanimous forgiveness.

* * *

And then had come the scourge, grinning and lethal, from the nightmare caverns of Tartarus. West and I had graduated about the time of its beginning, but had remained for additional work at the summer school, so were in Arkham when it broke with full daemoniac fury upon the town. Though not as yet licensed physicians, we now had our degrees, and were pressed into public service as the numbers of the stricken grew. The situation was almost past management, and deaths ensued too frequently for the local undertakers to handle. Burials without embalming were made in rapid succession, and even the Christchurch Cemetery receiving tomb was crammed with coffins of the unembalmed dead. This circumstance was not without effect on West, who thought often of the irony of the situation: so many fresh specimens, yet none for his persecuted researches! We were frightfully overworked, and the terrific mental and nervous strain made my friend brood morbidly.

But West's gentle enemies were no less harassed with prostrating duties. College had all but closed, but every doctor of the medical faculty was helping to fight the typhoid plague. Dr. Halsey in particular had distinguished himself in sacrificing service, applying his extreme skill with wholehearted energy to cases which many others shunned because of danger or apparent hopelessness. Before a month was over the fearless dean had become a popular hero, though he seemed unconscious of his fame as he struggled to keep from collapsing with physical fatigue and nervous exhaustion. West could not withhold admiration for the fortitude of his foe, but because of this was even more determined to prove to him the truth of his amazing doctrines. Taking advantage of the disorganisation of both college work and municipal health regulations, he managed to get a recently deceased body smuggled into the university dissecting-room one night, and in my presence injected a new modification of his solution. The thing actually opened its eyes, but only stared at the ceiling with a look of soul-petrifying horror before collapsing into an inertness from which nothing could rouse it. West said it was not fresh enough; the hot summer air does not favour corpses. That time we were almost caught before incinerating the thing, and West doubted the advisability of repeating his daring misuse of the college laboratory.

The peak of the epidemic was reached in August. West and I were almost dead, and Dr. Halsey did die on the 14th. The students all attended the hasty funeral on the 15th, and bought an impressive wreath, though the latter was quite overshadowed by the tributes sent by wealthy Arkham citizens and by the municipality itself. It was almost a public affair, for the dean had surely been a public benefactor. After the entombment we were all somewhat depressed and spent the afternoon at the bar of the Commercial House, where West, though shaken by the death of his chief opponent, chilled the rest of us with references of his notorious theories. Most of the students went home, or to various duties, as the evening advanced, but West persuaded me to aid him in "making a night of it." West's landlady saw us arrive at his room about two in the morning, with a third man between us; and she told her husband we had evidently dined and wined rather well. Apparently this acidulous matron was right, for about 3 A.M. the whole house was aroused by cries coming from West's room, where when they broke down the door they found the two of us unconscious on the blood-stained carpet; beaten, scratched and mauled, with the broken remnants of West's bottles and instruments around us. Only an open window told what had become of our assailant, and many wondered how he himself had fared after the terrific leap from the second storey to the lawn which he must have made. There were some strange garments in the room, but West upon regaining consciousness said they did not belong to the stranger, but were specimens collected for bacteriological analysis in the course of investigations in the transmission of germ diseases. He ordered them burnt as soon as possible in the capacious fireplace. To the police we both declared ignorance of our late companion's identity. He was, West nervously said, a congenial stranger whom we had met at some downtown bar of uncertain location. We had all been rather jovial, and West and I did not wish to have our pugnacious companion hunted down.

* * *

That same night saw the beginning of the second Arkham horror—the horror that to me eclipsed the plague itself. Christchurch Cemetery was the scene of a terrible killing; a watchman having been clawed to death in a manner not only too hideous for description, but raising a doubt as to the human agency of the deed. The victim had been seen alive considerably after midnight—the dawn revealed the unutterable thing. The manager of a circus at the neighboring town of Bolton was questioned, but he swore no beast had at any time escaped from its cage. Those who found the body noted a trail of blood leading to the receiving tomb, where a small pool of red lay on the concrete just outside the gate. A fainter trail led away toward the woods, but it soon gave out.

The next night devils danced on the roofs of Arkham, and unnatural madness howled in the wind. Through the fevered town had crept a curse which some said was greater than the plague, and which some whispered was the embodied daemon-soul of the plague itself. Eight houses were entered by a nameless thing which strewed red death in its wake—in all, seventeen maimed and shapeless remnants of bodies were left behind by the voiceless, sadistic monster that crept abroad. A few persons had half seen it in the dark, and said it was white and like a malformed ape or anthropomorphic fiend. It had not left behind quite all that it had attacked, for sometimes it had been hungry. The number it had killed was fourteen; three of the bodies had been in stricken homes and had not been alive.

On the third night frantic bands of searchers, led by the police, captured it in a house on Crane Street near the Miskatonic campus. They had organised the quest with care, keeping in touch by means of volunteer telephone stations, and when someone in the college district reported hearing a scratching at a shuttered window, the net was quickly spread. On account of the general alarm and precautions there were only two more victims, and the capture was effected without major causalities. The thing was finally stopped by a bullet, though not a fatal one, and was rushed to the local hospital amidst universal excitement and loathing.

For it had been a man. This much was clear despite the nauseous eyes, the voiceless simianism, and the daemonic savagery. They dressed its wound and carted it to the asylum at Sefton, where it beat its head against the walls of a padded cell for sixteen years—until the recent mishap, when it escaped under circumstances few like to mention. What had most disgusted the searchers of Arkham was the thing they noticed when the monster's face was cleaned—the mocking, unbelievable resemblance to a learned and self-sacrificing martyr who had been entombed but three days before—the late Dr. Allan Halsey, public benefactor and dean of the medical school Miskatonic University.

To the vanished Herbert West and to me the disgust and horror were supreme. I shudder tonight as I think of it; shudder even more than I did that morning when West muttered through his bandages:

"Damn it, it wasn't *quite* fresh enough!"

"…he hoped to uncover the secret of life and restore to perpetual animation the graveyard's cold clay."

SIX SHOTS BY MOONLIGHT

It is uncommon to fire all six shots of a revolver with great suddenness when one would probably be sufficient, but many things in the life of Herbert West were uncommon. It is, for instance, not often a young physician leaving college is obliged to conceal the principles which guide his selection of a home and office, yet that was the case with Herbert West. When he and I obtained our degrees at the medical school of Miskatonic University, and sought to relieve our poverty by setting up as general practitioners, we took great care not to say we chose our house because it was fairly well isolated, and as near as possible to the potter's field.

Reticence such as this is seldom without a cause, nor indeed was ours, for our requirements were those resulting from a life-work distinctly unpopular. Outwardly we were doctors only, but beneath the surface were aims of far greater and more terrible moment—for the essence of Herbert West's existence was a quest amid black and forbidden realms of the unknown, in which he hoped to uncover the secret of life and restore to perpetual animation the graveyard's cold clay. Such a quest demands strange materials, among them fresh human bodies, and in order to keep supplied with these indispensible things one must live quietly and not far from a place of informal interment.

* * *

West and I had met in college, and I had been the only one to sympathise with his hideous experiments. Gradually I had come to be his inseparable assistant, and now that we were out of college we had to keep together. It was not easy to find a good opening for two doctors in company, but finally the influence of the university secured us a practice in Bolton, a factory town near Arkham, the seat of the college. The Bolton Worsted Mills are the largest in the Miskatonic Valley, and their polyglot employees are never popular as patients with the local physicians. We chose our house with the greatest care, seizing at last on a rather run-down cottage near the end of Pond Street; five numbers from the closest neighbour, and separated from the local potter's field by only a stretch of meadow land, bisected by a narrow neck of rather dense forest which lies to the north. The distance was greater than we wished, but we could get no nearer house without going on the other side of the field, wholly out of the factory district. We were not much displeased, however, since there were no people between us and our sinister source of supplies. The walk was a trifle long, but we could haul our silent specimens undisturbed.

Our practice was surprisingly large from the very first—large enough to please most young doctors, and large enough to be a bore and a burden to students whose real interest lay elsewhere. The mill-hands were of somewhat turbulent inclinations, and besides their many natural needs, their frequent clashes and stabbing affrays gave us plenty to do. But what actually absorbed our minds was the secret laboratory we had fitted up in the cellar—the laboratory with the long table under the electric lights, where in the small hours of the morning we often injected West's various solutions into the veins of the things we dragged from the potter's field. West was experimenting madly to find something which would start man's vital motions anew after they had been stopped by the thing we call death, but had encountered ghastly obstacles. The solution had to be differently compounded for different types. What would serve for guinea-pigs would not serve for human beings, and different human specimens required large modifications.

The bodies had to be exceedingly fresh, or the slight decomposition of brain tissue would render perfect reanimation impossible. Indeed, the greatest problem was to get them fresh enough. West had had horrible experiences during his secret college researches with corpses of doubtful vintage. The results of partial or imperfect animation were much more hideous than were the total failures, and we both held fearsome recollections of such things. Ever since our first daemonic session in the deserted farmhouse on Meadow Hill in Arkham, we had felt a brooding menace; and West, though a calm, blond, blue-eyed scientific automaton in most respects, often confessed to a shuddering sensation of stealthy pursuit. He half felt he was being followed—a psychological delusion of shaken nerves, enhanced by the undeniably disturbing fact that at least one of our reanimated specimens was still alive: a frightful, carnivorous thing in a padded cell at Sefton. Then there was another—our first— whose exact fate we had never learned.

We had fair luck with specimens in Bolton—much better than in Arkham. We had not been settled a week before we got an accident victim on the very night of burial, making it open its eyes with an amazingly rational expression before the solution failed. It had lost an arm, and if it had been a perfect body we might have succeeded better. Between then and the next January we secured three more: one total failure, one case of marked muscular motion, and one rather shivery thing which rose of itself and uttered a sound. Then came a period came a period when luck was poor. Interments fells off, and those that did occur were poor specimens either too diseased or too maimed for use. We kept track of all deaths and their circumstances with systematic care.

* * *

One March night, however, we unexpectedly obtained a specimen which did not come from the potter's field. In Bolton the prevailing spirit of Puritanism had outlawed the sport of boxing, with the usual result. Surreptitious and ill-conducted bouts among the mill-workers were common, and occasionally professional talent of low grade was imported. This late winter night there had been such a match; evidently with disastrous results, since two timorous Poles had come to us with incoherently whispered entreaties to attend to a very secret and desperate case. We followed them to an abandoned barn, where the remnants of a crowd of frightened foreigners were watching a silent black form on the floor.

The match had been between Kid O'Brine—a lubberly and now quacking youth with a most un-Hibernian hooked nose—and Buck Robinson, *The Harlem Smoke*. The Negro had been knocked out, and a moment's examination shewed us he would permanently remain so. He was a loathsome, gorilla-like thing, with abnormally long arms which I could not help calling forelegs, and a face that conjured up thoughts of unspeakable Congo secrets and tom-tom poundings under an eery moon. The body must have looked worse in life, but the world holds many ugly things. Fear was upon the whole pitiful crowd, for they know what the law would exact of them, if the affair were not hushed up; and they were therefore very grateful when West, in spite of my involuntary shudders, offered to get rid of the thing quietly, for a purpose I knew all too well.

There was bright moonlight over the snowless landscape, but we dressed the thing and carried it home between us through the deserted streets and meadows, as we had carried a similar thing one horrible night in Arkham. We approached the house from the field in the rear, took the specimen in the back door and down the cellar stairs, and prepared it for the usual experiment. Our fear of the police was absurdly great, though we had timed our trip to avoid the solitary policeman of that section.

The result was wearily anticlimactic. Ghastly as our prize appeared, it was wholly unresponsive to every solution we injected into its black arm; solutions prepared from experiments with white specimens only. So as the hour grew dangerously near to dawn we did as we had done with the others, dragging the thing across the meadows to the neck of the woods near the potter's field, burying it in the best sort of grave the frozen ground would furnish. The grave was not very deep, but fully as good as that of the previous specimen (the thing that had uttered a sound). In the light of our dark lanterns we carefully covered it with leaves and dead vines, fairly certain the police would never find it in a forest so dim and dense.

* * *

The next day I was increasingly apprehensive about the police, for a patient brought rumours of a suspected fight and death. West had still another source of worry, for he had been called in the afternoon to a case which ended very threateningly. An Italian woman had become hysterical over her missing child—a lad of five who had strayed off early in the morning and failed to appear for dinner—and had developed symptoms highly alarming in view of an always weak heart. It was a very foolish hysteria, for the boy had often run away before; but Italian peasants are exceedingly superstitious, and this woman seemed as much harassed by omens as by facts. About seven o'clock in the evening she had died, and her frantic husband had made a frightful scene in his efforts to kill West, whom he wildly blamed for not saving her life. Friends had held him when he drew a stiletto, but West had departed amidst his inhuman shrieks, curses and oaths of vengeance. In his latest affliction the fellow seemed to have forgotten his child, who was still missing as the night advanced. There was some talk of searching the woods, but most of the family's friends were busy with the dead woman and the screaming man. Altogether, the nervous strain upon West must have been tremendous. Thoughts of the police and the mad Italian both weighed heavily.

We retired about eleven, but I did not sleep well. Bolton had a surprisingly good police force for so small a town, and I could not help fearing the mess which would ensue if the affair of the night before were ever tracked down. It might mean the end of all our local work and perhaps prison for both West and me. I did not like these rumours of a fight which were floating about. After the clock had struck three the moon shone in my eyes, but I turned over without rising to pull down the shade. Then came the steady rattling at the back door.

I lay still and somewhat dazed, but before long I heard West's rap on my door. He was clad in dressing gown and slippers, and had in his hands a revolver and an electric flashlight. From the revolver I knew he was thinking more of the crazed Italian than of the police.

"We'd better both go," he whispered. "It wouldn't do not to answer it anyway, and it might be a patient—it would be like one of those fools to try the back door."

So we both went down the stairs on tiptoe, with a fear partly justified and partly which comes only from the soul during the weird small hours. The rattling continued, growing somewhat louder. When we reached the door I cautiously unbolted it and threw it open, and as the moon streamed revealingly down on the form silhouetted there, West did a peculiar thing. Despite the obvious danger of attracting notice and bringing down on our heads the dreaded police investigation—a thing which after all was mercifully averted by the relative isolation of our cottage—my friend suddenly, excitedly and unnecessarily emptied all six chambers of his revolver into the nocturnal visitor.

For that visitor was neither Italian nor policeman. Looming hideously against the spectral moon was a gigantic misshapen thing not to be imagined save in nightmares—a glassy-eyed, ink-black apparition nearly on all fours, covered with bits of mould, leaves and vines, foul with caked blood, and having between its glistening white teeth a snow-white, terrible, cylindrical object terminating in a tiny hand.

"…natural life must be extinct, and the specimens
must be very fresh, but genuinely dead."

THE SCREAM OF THE DEAD

The scream of a dead man gave to me that acute and added horror of Dr. Herbert West which harassed the latter years of our companionship. It is natural such a thing as a dead man's screaming should give horror; for it is obviously not a pleasing or ordinary occurrence; but I was used to similar experiences, hence suffered on this occasion only because of a particular circumstance. And, as I have implied, it was not of the dead man himself I became afraid.

* * *

Herbert West, whose associate and assistant I was, possessed scientific interests far beyond the usual routine of a village physician. That was why, when establishing his practice in Bolton, he had chosen an isolated house near the potter's field. Briefly and brutally stated, West's sole absorbing interest was a secret study of the phenomena of life and its cessation, leading toward the reanimation of the dead through injections of an excitant solution. For this ghastly experimenting it was necessary to have a constant supply of very fresh human bodies; very fresh because even the least decay hopelessly damaged the brain structure, and human because we found the solution had to be compounded differently for different types of organisms. Scores of rabbits and guinea-pigs had been killed and treated, but their trail was a blind one. West had never fully succeeded because he had never been able to secure a corpse sufficiently fresh. What he wanted were bodies from which vitality had only just departed; bodies with every cell intact and capable of receiving again the impulse toward the mode of motion called life. There was hope this second and artificial life might be made perpetual by repetitions of the injection, but we had learned an ordinary natural life would not respond to the action. To establish the artificial motion, natural life must be extinct, and the specimens must be very fresh, but genuinely dead.

The awesome quest had begun when West and I were students at the Miskatonic University Medical School in Arkham, vividly conscious for the first time of the thoroughly mechanical nature of life. That was seven years before, but West looked scarcely a day older now. He was small, blond, clean-shaven, soft-voiced and spectacled, with only an occasional flash of a cold blue eye to tell of the hardening and growing fanaticism of his character the pressure of his terrible investigations. Our experiences had often been hideous in the extreme; the results of defective reanimation, when lumps of graveyard clay had been galvanised into morbid, unnatural and brainless motion by various modifications of the vital solution.

One thing had uttered a nerve-shattering scream; another had risen violently, beaten us both to unconsciousness, and run amuck in a shocking way before it could be placed behind asylum bars; still another, a loathsome African monstrosity, had clawed out of its shallow grave and done a deed (West had had to shoot that object). We could not get bodies fresh enough to shew any trace of reason when reanimated, so had perforce created nameless horrors. It was disturbing to think one, perhaps two, or our monsters still lived—that thought haunted us shadowingly, till finally West disappeared under frightful circumstances. But at the time of the scream in the cellar laboratory of the isolated Bolton cottage, our fears were subordinate to our anxiety for extremely fresh specimens. West was more avid than I, so it almost seemed to me he looked half-covetously at any very healthy living physique.

* * *

It was in July, 1910, that the bad luck regarding specimens began to turn. I had been on a long visit to my parents in Illinois, and upon my return found West in a state of singular elation. He had, he told me excitedly, in all likelihood solved the problem of freshness through an approach from an entirely new angle—that of artificial preservation. I had known he was working on a new and highly unusual embalming compound, and was not surprised it had turned out well; but until he explained the details I was rather puzzled as to how such a compound could help our work, since the objectionable staleness of the specimens was largely due to delay occurred before we secured them. This, I now saw, West clearly recognised; creating his embalming compound for future rather than immediate use, and trusting to fate to supply again some very recent and unburied corpse, as it had years before when we obtained the Negro killed in the Bolton prize-fight. At last fate had been kind, so on this occasion there lay in the secret cellar laboratory a corpse whose decay could not by any possibility have begun. What would happen on reanimation, and whether we could hope for a revival of mind and reason, West did not venture to predict. The experiment would be landmark in our studies, and he had saved the new body for my return, so both of us might share the spectacle in an accustomed fashion.

West told me how he had obtained the specimen. It had been a vigorous man; a well-dressed stranger just off the train on his way to transact some business with the Bolton Worsted Mills. The walk through town had been long, and by the time the traveler paused at our cottage to ask the way to the factories he heart had become greatly overtaxed. He had refused a stimulant, and had suddenly dropped dead only a moment later. The body, as might be expected, seemed to West a heaven-sent gift. In his brief conversation the stranger had made it clear he was unknown in Bolton, and a search of his pockets subsequently revealed him to be one Robert Leavitt of St. Louis, apparently without a family to make instate inquiries about his disappearance. If this man could not be restored to life, no one would know of our experiment. We buried our materials in a dense strip of woods between the house and the potter's field. If, on the other hand, he could be restored, our fame would be brilliantly and perpetually established. So without delay West had injected into the body's wrist the compound which would hold it fresh for use after my arrival. The mater of the presumably weak heart, which to my mind imperiled the success of our experiment, did not appear to trouble West extensively. He hoped at last to obtain what he had never obtained before—a rekindled spark of reason and perhaps a normal-living creature.

So on the night of July 18, 1910, Herbert West and I stood in the cellar laboratory and gazed at a white, silent figure beneath the dazzling arc-light. The embalming compound had worked uncannily well, for as I stared fascinatedly at the sturdy frame which had lain two weeks without stiffening I was moved to seek West's assurance the thing was really dead. This assurance he gave readily enough, reminding me the reanimating solution was never used without careful tests as to life, since it could have no effect if any of the original vitality were present. As West proceeded to take preliminary steps, I was impressed by the vast intricacy of the experiment; an intricacy so vast he could trust no hand less delicate than his own. Forbidding me to touch the body, he first injected a drug in the wrist just beside the place his needle had punctured when injected the embalming compound. This, he said, was to neutralise the compound and release the system to a normal relaxation so the reanimating solution might freely work when injected. Slightly later, when a change and a gentle tremor seemed to affect the dead limbs, West stuffed a pillow-like object violently over the twitching face, not withdrawing it until the corpse appeared quiet and ready for our attempt at reanimation. The pale enthusiast now applied some last perfunctory tests for absolute lifelessness, withdrew satisfied, and finally injected into the left arm an accurately measured amount of the vital elixir, prepared during the afternoon with a greater care than we had used since college days, when our feats were new and groping. I cannot express the wild, breathless suspense with which we waited for results on this first really fresh specimen—the first we could reasonably expect to open its lips in rational speech, perhaps to tell of what it had seen beyond the unfathomable abyss.

West was a materialist, believing in no soul and attributing all the workings of consciousness to bodily phenomena; consequently he looked for no revelations of hideous secrets from gulfs and caverns beyond death's barrier. I did not wholly disagree with him theoretically, yet held vague instinctive remnants of the primitive faith of my forefathers; so I could not help eyeing the corpse with a certain amount of awe and terrible expectation. Besides, I could not extract from my memory that hideous inhuman shriek we heard on the night we tried our first experiment in the deserted farmhouse at Arkham.

Very little time had elapsed before I saw the attempt was not to be a total failure. A touch of colour came to cheeks hitherto chalk-white, and spread out under the curiously ample stubble of sandy beard. West, who had his hand on the pulse of the left wrist, suddenly nodded significantly; and almost simultaneously a mist appeared on the mirror inclined above the body's mouth. There followed a few spasmodic muscular motions, and then an audible breathing and visible motion of the chest. I looked at the closed eyelids, and thought I detected a quivering. Then the lids opened, shewing eyes which were grey, calm and alive, but still unintelligent and not even curious.

In a moment of fantastic whim I whispered questions to the reddening ears; questions of other worlds of which the memory might still be present. Subsequent terror drove them from my mind, but I think the last one, which I repeated, was: "Where have you been?" I do not yet know whether I was answered or not, for no sound came from the well-shaped mouth; but I do know at that moment I firmly thought the thin lips moved silently, forming syllables which I would have vocalised as "only now" if that phrase had possessed any sense or relevancy. At that moment, as I say, I was elated with the conviction that the one great goal had been attained; and that for the first time a reanimated corpse had uttered distinct words impelled by actual reason. In the next moment there was no doubt about the triumph; no doubt the solution has truly accomplished, at least temporarily, its full mission of restoring rational and articulate life to the dead. But in triumph there came to me the greatest of all horrors—not horror of the thing that spoke, but of the deed I had witnessed and of the man with whom my professional fortunes were joined.

For that very fresh body, at last writhing into full and terrifying consciousness with eyes dilated at the memory of its last scene on earth, threw out its frantic hands in a life and death struggle with the air; and suddenly collapsing into a second and final dissolution from which there could be no return, screamed out the cry that will ring eternally in my aching brain:

"Help! Keep off, you cursed little tow-head fiend—keep that damned needle away from me!"

*"Gradually I came to find Herbert West himself
more horrible than anything he did…"*

THE HORROR FROM THE SHADOWS

Many men have related hideous things, not mentioned in print, which happened on the battlefields of the Great War. Some of these things have made me faint, others have convulsed me with devastating nausea, while still others have made me tremble and look behind me in the dark; yet despite the worst of them I believe I can relate the most hideous thing of all—the shocking, the unnatural, the unbelievable horror from the shadows.

* * *

In 1915 I was a physician with the rank of lieutenant in a Canadian regiment in Flanders, one of many Americans to precede the government itself into the gigantic struggle. I had not entered the army of my own initiative, but rather as a natural result of the enlistment of the man whose indispensable assistant I was—the celebrated Boston surgical specialist, Dr. Herbert West. Dr. West had been avid for a chance to serve as a surgeon in a great war, and when the chance had come he carried me with him almost against my will. There were reasons why I would have been glad to let the war separate us; reasons why I found the practice of medicine and the companionship of West more and more irritating; but when he had gone to Ottawa and through a colleague's influence secured a medical commission as a major, I could not resist the imperious persuasion of one determined I should accompany him in my usual capacity.

When I say Dr. West was avid to serve in battle I do not mean to imply he was either naturally warlike or anxious for the safety of civilization. Always an ice-bold intellectual machine; slight, blond, blue-eyed and spectacled; I think he secretly sneered at my occasional martial enthusiasm and censures of supine neutrality. There was, however, something he wanted in embattled Flanders; and in order to secure it had to assume a military exterior. What he wanted was not a thing which many persons want, but something connected with the peculiar branch of medical science which he had chosen quite clandestinely to follow, and in which he had achieved amazing and occasionally hideous results. It was, in fact, nothing more or less than an abundant supply of freshly killed men in every state of dismemberment.

Herbert West needed fresh bodies because his life-work was the reanimation of the dead. This work was not known to the fashionable clientele who had so swiftly built up his fame after his arrival in Boston; but was only too well known to me, who had been his closest friend and sole assistant since the old days in Miskatonic University Medical School at Arkham. It was in those college days that he had begun his terrible experiments, first on small animals and then on human bodies shockingly obtained. There was a solution which he injected into the veins of dead things, and if they were fresh enough they responded in strange ways. He had had much trouble in discovering the proper formula, for each type of organism was found to need a stimulus especially adapted to it. Terror stalked him when he reflected on his partial failures; nameless things resulting from imperfect solutions or from bodies insufficiently fresh. A certain number of these failures had remained alive—one was in an asylum while others had vanished—and as he thought conceivable yet impossible eventualities he often shivered beneath his usual stolidity.

West had soon learned absolute freshness was the prime requisite for useful specimens, and had accordingly resorted to frightful and unnatural expedients in body-snatching. In college, and during our early practice together in the factory town of Bolton, my attitude toward him had been largely one of fascinated interest; but as his boldness in methods grew, I began to develop a gnawing fear. I did like the way he looked at healthy living bodies; and then there came a nightmarish session in the cellar laboratory when I learned a certain specimen had been a living body when he secured it. That was the first time he had ever been able to revive the quality of rational thought in a corpse; and his success, obtained at such a loathsome cost, had completely hardened him.

Of his methods in the intervening five years I dare not speak. I was held to him by sheer force of fear, and witnessed sights no human tongue could repeat. Gradually I came to find Herbert West himself more horrible than anything he did—that was when it dawned on me his once normal scientific zeal for prolonging life had subtly degenerated into a mere morbid and ghoulish curiosity and secret sense of charnel picturesqueness. His interest had become a hellish and perverse addiction to the repellently and fiendishly abnormal; he gloated calmly over artificial monstrosities which would make most healthy men drop dead from fright and disgust; he became, behind his pallid intellectuality, a fastidious Baudelaire of physical experiment—a languid Elagabalus of the tombs.

Dangers he met unflinchingly; crimes he committed unmoved. I think the climax came when he had proved his point that rational life can be restored, and had sought new worlds to conquer by experimenting on the reanimation of detached parts of bodies. He had wild and original ideas on the independent vital properties of organic cells and nerve-tissue separated from natural physiological systems; and achieved some hideous preliminary results in the form of never-dying, artificially nourished tissue obtained from the nearly-hatched eggs of an indescribable tropical reptile. Two biological points he was exceedingly anxious to settle: first, whether any amount of consciousness and rational action was possible without the brain, proceeding from the spinal cord and various nerve-centres; and second, whether any kind of ethereal, intangible relation distinct from the maternal cells may exist to link the surgically separated parts of what has previously been a single living organism. All this research work required a prodigious supply of freshly slaughtered human flesh, and that was why Herbert West had entered the Great War.

* * *

The phantasmal, unmentionable thing occurred one midnight late in March, 1915, in a field hospital behind the lines of St. Eloi. I wonder even now if it could have been other than a daemoniac dream of delirium. West had a private laboratory in an east room of the barn-like temporary edifice, assigned him on his plea he was devising new and radical methods of the treatment of hitherto hopeless cases of maiming. There he worked like a butcher in the midst of his gory wares—I could never get used to the levity with which he handled and classified certain things. At times he actually did perform marvels of surgery for the soldiers; but his chief delights were of less public and philanthropic kind, requiring many explanations of sounds which seemed peculiar even amidst the babel of the damned. Among these sounds were frequent revolver shots—surely not uncommon on a battlefield, but distinctly uncommon in an hospital. Dr. West's reanimated specimens were not meant for long existence or a large audience. Beside human tissue, West employed much of the reptile embryo tissue which he had cultivated with such singular results; it was better than human material for maintaining life in organless fragments, and that was no my friend's chief activity. In a dark corner of the laboratory, over a queer incubating burner, he kept a large covered vat full of this reptilian cell-matter, which multiplied and grew puffily and hideously.

On the night of which I speak we had a splendid new specimen—a man at once physically powerful and of such high mentality that a sensitive nervous system was assured. It was rather ironic, for he was the officer who had helped West to his commission, and who was not to have been our associate. Moreover, he had in the past secretly studied the theory of reanimation to some extent under West. Major Sir Eric Moreland Clapham-Lee, D.S.O. was the greatest surgeon in our division, and had been hastily assigned to the St. Eloi sector when news of the heavy fighting reached headquarters. He had come in an aeroplane piloted by the intrepid Lieut. Ronald Hill, only to be shot down when directly over his destination. The fall had been spectacular and awful; Hill was unrecognisable afterward, but the wreck yielded up the great surgeon in a nearly decapitated but otherwise intact condition. West greedily seized the lifeless thing which had once been his friend and fellow scholar; and I shuddered when he finished severing the head, place it in his hellish vat of pulp reptile-tissue to preserve it for future experiments, and proceeded to treat the decapitated body on the operating table. He injected new blood, joined certain veins, arteries and nerves at the headless neck, and closed the ghastly aperture with engrafted skin from an unidentified specimen which had borne an officer's uniform. I knew what he wanted—to see if this highly organised body could exhibit, without its head, any of the signs of mental life which had distinguished Sir Eric Moreland Clapham-Lee. Once a student of reanimation, this silent trunk was now gruesomely called upon to exemplify it.

I can still see Herbert West under the sinister electric light as he injected his reanimating solution into the arm of the headless body. The scene I cannot describe—I should faint if I tried, for there is madness in a room full of classified charnel things, with blood and lesser human debris almost ankle deep on the slimy floor, and with hideous reptilian abnormalities sprouting, bubbling and baking over a winking bluish-green spectre of dim flame in a corner of black shadows.

The specimen, as West repeatedly observed, had a splendid nervous system. Much was expected of it; and as a few twitching motions began to appear, I could see the feverish interest in West's face. He was ready, I think, to see proof of his increasingly strong opinion that consciousness, reason and personality can exist independently of the brain—that man has no central connective spirit, but is merely a machine of nervous matter, each section more or less complete in itself. In one triumphant demonstration West was about to relegate the mystery of life to the category of myth. The body now twitched more vigorously, and beneath our avid eyes commenced to heave in a frightful way. The arms stirred disquietingly, the legs drew up, and various muscles contracted in a repulsive kind of writhing. Then the headless thing threw out its arms in a gesture which was unmistakably one of desperation—an intelligent desperation apparently sufficient to prove every theory of Herbert West. Certainly, the nerves were recalling the man's last act in life; the struggle to get free of the falling aeroplane.

What followed, I shall never positively know. It may have been wholly an hallucination from the shock caused at that instant by the sudden and complete destruction of the building in a cataclysm of German shellfire—who can gainsay it, since West and I were the only proved survivors? West liked to think that before his recent disappearance, but there were times when he could not; for it was queer we both had the same hallucination. The hideous occurrence itself was very simple, notable only for what it implied.

The body on the table had risen with a blind and terrible groping, and we had heard a sound. I should not call that sound a voice, for it was too awful. And yet its timbre was not the most awful thing about it. Neither was its message—it merely screamed, "Jump, Ronald, for God's sake, jump!" The awful thing was its source.

For it had come from the large covered vat in that ghoulish corner of crawling black shadows.

"He had slowly tried to perfect a solution which, injected into the veins of the newly deceased, would restore life…"

THE TOMB-LEGIONS

When Dr. Herbert West disappeared a year ago, the Boston police questioned me closely. They suspected I was holding something back, and perhaps suspected even graver things; but I could not tell them the truth because they would not have believed it. They knew, indeed, West had been connected with activities beyond the credence of ordinary men; for his hideous experiments in the reanimation of dead bodies had long been too extensive to admit of perfect secrecy; but the final soul-shattering catastrophe held elements of daemoniac phantasy which make even me doubt the reality of what I saw.

* * *

I was West's closet's friend and only confidential assistant. We had met years before, in medical school, and from the first I had shared his terrible researches. He had slowly tried to perfect a solution which, injected into the veins of the newly deceased, would restore life; a labour demanding an abundance of fresh corpses and therefore involving the most unnatural actions. Still more shocking were the products of some of the experiments—grisly masses of flesh that had been dead, but that West waked to a blind, brainless, nauseous animation. These were the usual results, for in order to reawaken the mind it was necessary to have specimens so absolutely fresh no decay could possibly affect the delicate brain-cells

This need for very fresh corpses had been West's moral undoing. They were hard to get, and one awful day he had secured his specimen when it was still alive and vigorous. A struggle, a needle and a powerful alkaloid had transformed it to a very fresh corpse, and the experiment had succeeded for a brief and memorable moment; but West had emerged with a soul calloused and seared, and a hardened eye which sometimes glanced with a kind of hideous and calculating appraisal at men of especially sensitive brain and especially vigorous physique. Toward the last I became acutely afraid of West, for he began to look at me that way. People did not seem to notice his glances, but they noticed my fear; and after his disappearance used that as a basis for some absurd suspicions.

West, in reality, was more afraid than I for his abominable pursuits entailed a life of furtiveness and dread of every shadow. Partly it was the police he feared; but sometimes his nervousness was deeper and more nebulous, touching on certain indescribable things into which he had injected a morbid life, and from which he had not seen that life depart. He usually finished his experiments with a revolver, but a few times he had not been quick enough. There was that first specimen on whose rifled grave marks of clawing were later seen. There was that Arkham professor's body which had done cannibal things before it had been captured and thrust unidentified into a madhouse cell at Sefton, where it beat the walls for sixteen years. Most of the other possibly surviving results were things less easy to speak of—for in later years West's scientific zeal had degenerated to an unhealthy and fantastic mania, and he had spent his chief skill in vitalising not entire human bodies but isolated parts of bodies, or parts joined to organic matter other than human. It had become fiendishly disgusting by the time he disappeared; many of the experiments could not even be hinted at in print. The

Great War, through which both of us served as surgeons, had intensified this side of West.

In saying West's fear of his specimens was nebulous, I have in mind particularly its complex nature. Part of it came merely from knowing of the existence of such nameless monsters, while another part arouse from apprehension of the bodily harm they might under certain circumstances do him. Their disappearance added horror to the situation—of them all West knew the whereabouts of only one, the pitiful asylum thing. Then there was a more subtle fear—a very fantastic sensation resulting from a curious experiment in the Canadian Army in 1915. West, in the midst of a severe battle, had reanimated Major Sir Eric Moreland Clapham-Lee, D.S.O., a fellow-physician who knew about his experiments and could have duplicated them. The head had been removed, so that the possibilities of quasi-intelligent life in the trunk might be investigated. Just as the building was wiped out by a German shell, there had been a success. The trunk had moved intelligently; and, unbelievable to relate, we were both sickeningly sure that articulate sounds had come from the detached head as it lay in a shadowy corner of the laboratory. The shell had been merciful, in a way—but West could never feel as certain as he wished, that we two were the only survivors. He used to make shuddering conjectures about the possible actions of a headless physician with the power of reanimating the dead.

West's last quarters were in a venerable house of much elegance, overlooking one of the oldest burying grounds in Boston. He had chosen the place for purely symbolic and fantastically aesthetic reasons, since most of the interments were of the colonial period and therefore of little use to a scientist seeking very fresh bodies. The laboratory was in a sub-cellar secretly constructed by imported workmen, and contained a huge incinerator for the quite and complete disposal of such bodies, or fragments and synthetic mockeries of bodies, as might remain from the morbid experiments and unhallowed amusements of the owner. During the excavation of this cellar the workmen struck some exceedingly ancient masonry; undoubtedly connected with the old burying ground, yet far too deep to correspond with any known sepulcher therein. After a number of calculations West decided it represented some secret chamber beneath the tomb of the Averills, where the last interment had been made in 1768. I was with him when he studied the nitrous, dripping walls laid bare by the spades and mattocks of the men, and was prepared for the gruesome thrill which would attend the uncovering of centuried grave-secrets; but for the first time West's new timidity conquered his natural curiosity, and he betrayed his degenerating fibre by ordering the masonry left intact and plastered over. Thus it remained till that final hellish night; part of the walls of the secret laboratory. I speak of West's decadence, but must add it was a purely mental and intangible thing. Outwardly he was the same to the last—calm, cold, slight and yellow-haired, with spectacled blue eyes and a general aspect of youth which years and fears seemed never to change. He seemed calm even when he thought of that clawed grave and looked over his shoulder; even when he thought of the carnivorous thing that gnawed and pawed at Sefton bars.

* * *

The end of Herbert West began one evening in our joint study when he was dividing his curious glance between the newspaper and me. A strange headline item had struck at him from the crumpled pages, and a nameless titan claw had seemed to reach down through sixteen years. Something fearsome and incredible had happened at Sefton Asylum fifty miles away, stunning the neighbourhood and baffling the police. In the small hours of the morning a body of silent men had entered the grounds and their leader had aroused the attendants. He was a menacing military figure who talked without moving his lips and whose voice seemed almost ventriloquially connected with an immense black case he carried. His expressionless face was handsome to the point of radiant beauty, but had shocked the superintendant when the hall light fell upon it—for it was a wax face with eyes of painted glass. Some nameless accident had befallen this man. A larger man guided his steps; a repellent bulk whose bluish face seemed half eaten away from some unknown malady. The speaker had asked for the custody of the cannibal monster committed from Arkham sixteen years before; and upon being refused, gave a signal which precipitated a shocking riot. The fiends had beaten, trampled and bitten every attendant who did not flee, killing four before finally succeeding in the liberation of the monster. Those victims who could recall the event without hysteria swore the creatures had acted less like men than like unthinkable automata guided by the wax-faced leader. By the time help could be summoned, every trace of the men and of their mad charge had vanished.

From the hour of reading this item until midnight, West sat almost paralysed. At midnight the doorbell rang, startling him fearfully. All the servants were asleep in the attic, so I answered the bell. As I have told the police, there was no wagon in the street; but only a group of strange-looking figures bearing a large square box which they deposited in the hallway after one of them had grunted in a highly unnatural voice, "Express—prepaid." They filed out of the house with a jerky tread, and as I watched them go I had an odd idea they were turning toward the ancient cemetery on which the back of the house abutted. When I slammed the door after them West came downstairs and looked at the box. It was about two feet square, and bore West's correct name and present address. It also bore the inscription, "From Eric Moreland Clapham-Lee, St. Eloi, Flanders." Six years before, in Flanders, a shelled hospital had fallen upon the headless reanimated trunk of Dr. Clapham-Lee, and upon the detached head which—perhaps—had uttered articulate sounds.

West was not even excited now. His condition was more ghastly. Quickly he said, "It's the finish—but let's incinerate—this." We carried the thing down to the laboratory—listening. I do not remember many particulars—you can imagine my state of mind—but it is a vicious lie to say it was Herbert West's body which I put into the incinerator. We both inserted the whole unopened wooden box, closed the door, and started the electricity. Nor did any sound come from the box, after all.

It was West who first noticed the falling plaster on that part of the wall where the ancient tomb masonry had been covered up. I was going to run, but he stopped me. Then I saw a small black aperture, felt a ghoulish wind of ice, and smelled the charnel bowels of putrescent earth. There was no sound, but just then the electric lights went out and I saw outlined against some phosphorescence of the nether world a horde of silent toiling things which only insanity—or worse—could create. Their outlines were human, semi-human, fractionally human and not human at all—the horde was grotesquely heterogeneous. They were removing the stones quietly, one by one, from the centuried wall. And then, as the breach became large enough, they came out into the laboratory in single file; led by a stalking thing with a beautiful head made of wax.

A sort of mad-eyed monstrosity behind the leader seized on Herbert West. West did not resist or utter a sound. Then they all sprang at him and tore him to pieces before my eyes, bearing the fragments away into that subterranean vault of fabulous abominations. West's head was carried off by the wax-headed leader, who wore a Canadian officer's uniform. As it disappeared I saw the blue eyes behind the spectacles hideously blazing with their first touch of frantic, visible emotion.

* * *

Servants found me unconscious in the morning. West was gone. The incinerator contained only unidentifiable ashes. Detectives have questioned me, but what can I say? The Sefton tragedy they will not connect with West; not that, nor the men with the box, whose existence they deny. I told them of the vault, and they pointed to the unbroken plaster wall and laughed. So I told them no more. They imply I am either a madman or a murderer—probably I am mad. But I might not be mad if those accursed tomb-legions had not been so silent.

Herbert West - Resurrected

THE EMPTY HOUSE ON HARLEY STREET

All of London is enthralled with Dr. Herbert.

Every day patients line up to be cured of their ails and specialists in all branches of medicine consult with him. Prominent spiritualists confer with him as well while the grieving come to ask about lost loved ones. A few folks have even claimed that Herbert resuscitated someone recently dead once or twice.

"Reanimating the dead? Preposterous!"

It does sound ludicrous, but rumors can be good for business so long as they do not take on a life of their own, so as Herbert's associate and spokesman I am always vigilant not to discourage the validity while pruning the voracity of such gossip.

Dr. Herbert may become a greater phenomenon than Franz Mesmer. Many people have indisputably benefited from seeing him, but I make sure nobody knows anything about him. It is critical—essential—that Herbert remain a blank canvas so people can make what they want of him. He never talks about himself or his past. His credentials are his knowledge and successes. Herbert has detractors and doubters, as great doctors and great conjure-men must, but so far no admonition or accusation can be heard over his accolades.

This grand old city has never seen anything like Dr. Herbert and odds are it never will again. I hope so, anyway, for reasons that may be good or awful.

* * *

I first made Herbert's acquaintance in a nightmare.

I had not been in London long, arriving late one winter after nearly being devoured by a rumor about me. I escaped America with my skin but not my reputation and needing to hide in a new country living a new kind of life

My new name is Levi Hip. My real name will remain my secret. I am revealing more than I care to already, beginning with that nightmare, which gave me no peace as it tugged at me like a divining rod. I have reason to suspect a few Londoners maybe suffered the same nightmare on the same night, but Fate or coincidence got me to Swain's Lane first where I was drawn to the Circle of Lebanon in Highgate Cemetery.

The only light at that late hour and that deep into the West Cemetery came from a waning crescent moon, but an ancient cedar obstructed its faint glimmer as I descended into that ring of tombs. This was not my first night-call on a graveyard so I brought along my flashlight, but I felt like a virgin pilgrim as I passed a procession of thresholds in the Egyptian style on the inner side and Classical on the outer, until the course was blocked by a mostly prone trilithon with an iron hatch jutting out of the ground. My mind painted the rusty whirls on the hatch's surface into imps and spawns skittering across cuneiforms of threatful knowledge, but I continued apace as the hatch warped like a hot cooking sheet doused in cold water, and dropped open to expose steps hewn from the bedrock banking far into the earth. I followed them down, unwilling to turn back. That's my excuse, anyway.

How many steps? Who knows? I lost count by the time I reached a rock-tomb with a wondrous curving ashlar wall of black khalkedon with white veins. The precision of the dress and the polish to the bricks was inhuman, and scrolled into this marvel by some Moving Finger was a name:

HERBERT WEST

My mind might have buckled under the absurdities of the moment if I hadn't been too busy fixating on the name, as anyone would have who is familiar with New England medicine. West graduated from the prestigious Miskatonic University Medical School, was a colleague of the late Sir Eric Moreland Clapham-Lee (D.S.O.), and served as a volunteer officer with the Canadian Army Medical Corps during the Great War. During his relatively short career in Boston, West had compiled a list of almost miraculous surgical successes along with a reputation for being obsessed with finding an excitant solution to revivify the dead, but about the time I abandoned the States I read West had apparently been murdered by his long-time associate.

I stared at that name on that wall. "This doesn't make sense."

What made even less sense was my growing compulsion to get at the other side of that wall. Something there needed to be released, but even if I had the proper tools the wall struck me as impregnable. I could feel no chink or weak spot as I ran my hands over the silky bricks, which were unexpectedly warm and almost moist, but as if guided by a hunch I pressed my palms against the brick with the "H," stepped back, and it slid back with me, easy and light as a drawer, releasing an effluence of queer light. I slid out more bricks, not able or wanting to stop despite seeing something like this in my nightmare. In that dream, some sort of ancient masonry had been deconstructed from behind as the same queer kind of light gushed out, along with a shambling legion of the damned. Was my nightmare turning into a premonition? I didn't believe in such things, but was anything happening believable? Only illumination escaped through my aperture, however, and as soon as I could slip through I did.

The candlepower was too much for me to make out any details of the other side.

All I could see for certain was Dr. Herbert West.

To say he was worse for wear is an understatement, and to say I was amazed he was alive much less conscious even more so. Instead of being afraid, though, I was fascinated, and I like to think we hit it off from the start.

"I need your help," Herbert said after I introduced myself. "There's somewhere I must be. Now."

An indefatigable fire kindled in his blue eyes. I admired that, given the circumstances.

"Well, I've come this far. In for a penny…"

* * *

Less than four miles north of Swain's Lane is Harley Street, a hub of medical practioners, surgeons, and hospitals, and a few doors down from the office of Edward Bach stands Agar House. No one had lived there since its owner died in the war, but Agar House was far from abandoned. Something watched over the place.

Herbert became my new divining rod after we left the cemetery, and he was adamant we enter the house unseen, so I found a narrow passage off an adjoining street that took us to a wooden gate that led into Agar House's deserted backyard. I would have picked the rear door's lock next, only it was open. "So much for sneaking in." I asked Herbert if he was still game for going inside.

"We've no choice."

We searched every room only to find furnishings playing spooks underneath white sheets blanketed with dust, but when we came to a circular consulting room it looked like I imagine it did when its owner was practicing here. On the desk an envelope was propped against an unlit candle. I made Herbert comfortable and then picked up the envelope. "This paper feels new." I started to open it until Herbert said, "Someone's here. I can feel it."

Footsteps coming straight towards us interrupted further talk. The consulting room had no windows or other exits. I had let us get cornered, and as much as it galled me all I could do now was wait and improvise.

A tall, brawny man with brown hair stepped into the room and blocked the door. He appeared young but struck me as old. His skin and gray eyes had a lackluster cast to them that "pale" doesn't accurately describe. He had handsome features and I deduced he was a laborer or used to be. The stranger recognized Herbert, who recognized him, but I couldn't tell which one made the other more anxious. There were no introductions. The stranger just asked Herbert in an odd high-pitched voice: "Why?"

I didn't understand the question and Herbert opted not to answer.

"Did you read the letter?"

"Not yet."

A pause, then the stranger repeated: "Why?"

I still had no idea what the man wanted to know, so I couldn't understand why Herbert suddenly looked a bit humbled, almost chastised. "I know you won't believe this, but my intentions were for the best."

"You meant no harm, Doctor?"

"No."

"So why not stop? You had to see the horrors you were making. Why not stop? You couldn't have thought you could ever make things right."

Herbert had trouble finding the right words, then settled on, "That didn't matter. I couldn't stop trying."

"Really? So then I suppose you never thought that a dead man might want to stay dead?"

"That's ridiculous."

"Is it? I drowned myself. Why would I want to come back?"

Herbert jerked. "You're no suicide."

"Oh, yes, I am. I was working alone on a bridge. As alone as I was in the world. I'd had enough. I let myself fall. I did my part. All you had to do was leave me dead."

"I didn't know. No one did." Herbert sounded sincere.

"Would that have mattered? You couldn't stop. Worse, you didn't care. You abandoned me."

"Not true! We thought you burned in the fire."

"I was more alone than ever! Wandering without the strength to die a second time. I never found that courage again. Then the Major came and gave me purpose. He gave everything like me purpose."

Whatever that meant got the better of Herbert. His chagrin vanished, incinerated by that indefatigable fire. "Yes. I'll never forget that night."

"And I bet you wanted to die, but you couldn't. The Major saw to that. How did that make you feel?"

"Like you in some ways, I imagine. Does that make you happy?" The stranger opted not to answer. "So what now?"

An unhappy grin sliced the stranger's lips. "Now it ends. My task is about done…I've asked you everything I've ever wanted…so why delay it?"

This was the first thing either of them had said I was pretty sure I understood. "No! Don't try it!" I needed to give the stranger a chance to change his mind, but he took one step towards Herbert, then a second, much faster than the first.

That cinched it.

Only fools visit graveyards following nightmares unarmed, and I'm not stupid. Gunfire draws attention, so I whipped the stranger's Adam's apple with a blackjack as he passed me. He clutched his throat and dropped to his knees. Killing a man is never pleasant and best for all if done quick, so I drew my stiletto, finished my task, then cleaned the knife on the back of his coat and used it to open the envelope, hoping for some answers about what was happening. What I read only rattled me more. "This letter says, 'Do with it what you will,' and it's signed 'Sir Eric Moreland Clapham-Lee, late.'" I sat and then stared at my companion. "I need answers."

"Are you sure about that? It's a long story. One you might not want to hear."

"I just saved your life! *Twice* if you count the cemetery! So don't pussyfoot unless you want me to leave."

"No, Levi, don't." He took a breath. "I will tell you all I can." But first he asked, "What do you suppose he means?"

"Who?"

"Clapham-Lee. What does he mean 'it'? Is he talking about that thing of the floor or this house of his?"

I hadn't considered that. "I suppose that depends if the note was meant for you or the dead man, don't you think?"

* * *

Herbert told me everything about his experiments in reanimation, starting with his college days to the night Clapham-Lee's tomb-legions shredded him. What started as a quest to ward away death had descended into obscenity. At the risk of repeating myself, to say Herbert West lost his way is an understatement. As for how he survived Clapham-Lee's attack in Boston and ended up in Highgate Cemetery, Herbert had no memories but did have a wonderful hypothesis.

"I can only describe it as *supranatural* radiation. Not supernatural, something beyond nature. I have to believe what I am experiencing is a part of nature, a power akin to cosmic rays that originate beyond our solar system yet can affect the Earth, or gamma radiation which can originate on our world. In either case this supranatural radiation, unlike ionizing radiation, is not biologically hazardous, but rather sustains life against all obstacles. It also appears that this radiation can be manipulated, which would explain how Clapham-Lee performed his assault on me, though that manipulation was crude at best. If I were more fanciful I might suggest this radiation is the basis for the legend of magic. But imagine what a radiation like this means to my research! This is not just a new approach; it's a virgin frontier offering limitless possibilities! And who better to blaze the trails then me, Levi? It's part of me. At times I can feel it like a heartbeat."

I won't deny that Herbert's hypothesis is outrageous, but I also find it intriguing. Its possibilities put the sideshow claims about snake oil and radium to shame, and the research will require years, maybe decades, giving Herbert and me a second chance at a productive life. Research is expensive, though, so we created Dr. Herbert to pay the bills. We also had to disguise the fact that all that remains of my new friend is his head, but for someone with my background it was a simple solution that added to the miraculous doctor's mystique. I decorated the wall and ceiling of Agar House's round consulting room with black velvet drapes, then situated a chair with a "body" behind a desk-like table in the center of the room. Dr. Herbert, "a quadriplegic," sits in this chair under a light aimed at his visitors but leaves him in relative darkness. It is a fitting sanctorum for a great doctor or great conjure-man or both, if I say so myself, and Dr. Herbert's success speaks for itself.

It might seem foolhardy to live and work in Agar House despite Clapham-Lee's potential invitation since the late Major may still harbor ill-will against Herbert, but we are convinced Clapham-Lee could find Herbert wherever he went to ground. Besides, staying in Agar House gives us a high ground, so to speak, to make ready for the day if Clapham-Lee and his tomb-legions try to strike again, plus we would probably never find a better place for our research.

One thing I have not revealed, even to Herbert, is my doubt about the supranatural nature of this radiation. Why couldn't it be supernatural? Or both?

I have visited the Circle of Lebanon again several times and the trilithon is never there. I suppose because it served its purpose, but what sort of radiation has a purpose? Doesn't that suggest a conscious attribute? It may be this radiation can only exist in certain loci, much like gamma radiation can only exist under certain high energy conditions like lightning strikes. That would explain why the tomb-legions delivered that box that West had presumed contained Clapham-Lee's head that last night in Boston. The Major knew Herbert would go to an incinerator in his sub-cellar to dispose of it, which placed Herbert near the ancient masonry I saw in my nightmare. A tomb on the other side of that masonry is probably a locus for the radiation that sustained Herbert during Clapham-Lee's attack, transported Herbert to London, and somehow continues to sustain him. I also have my doubts that Clapham-Lee's head was really in that box. I suspect it is sequestered in its own sanctorum, just as I suspect what remains of Herbert's body has been sequestered as well, perhaps as trophies or perhaps to draw Herbert away from Agar House if the need ever arises.

Yes, Herbert's hypothesis intrigues me, but it also worries me. We know so little about the radiation, most of all rather it is supranatural or supernatural. What kind of force are we dealing with? Like Herbert I can't stop myself from trying to find out, so I suppose some day we will discover the good or awful answer.

AUTHOR'S NOTE

So what do you think?

Is this a good direction for new adventures of Herbert West to continue? Disagree?

Don't just praise or kibitz! Keep the ball rolling! Get involved! Get up off the couch and go to the blogs and to the fan fiction sites! Write what you think about it, or better yet continue Herbert West's adventures! *You* tell the world what should happen next!

Who knows what the results will be, but you may never find a more rewarding experience.

Audio Script: "From the Dark"

CAST

HERBERT WEST: 20s, third-year medical student from Boston. Brilliant and arrogant, like a young Captain Von Trapp, but also haunted by an unspoken secret in his past that compels him to prove himself a better man than Death.

HUSTON SMITH: 20s, third-year medical student from Illinois. Intelligent, intrigued by West's theories, and increasingly overpowered by West's personality.

ORMOND SACKER: 20s, third year medical student. Provincial and conventional.

PROFESSOR HOLSTEIN: '60s, German, chemistry professor. Open-minded but realistic and strict.

DEAN HALSEY: 50s, New Englander, dean of Miskatonic University. Patient, wise, and conservative.

RICHARD POSNER: 20s, New Englander, laborer, drowned but got better. Well…sort of.

FX: **CICADAS WHINE UP AND UNDER**

FX: **SHOVELS DIGGING UP GRAVE DIRT**

FX: **WEST AND SMITH'S VOICES UNDER**

SMITH: How much more do we have to dig?

WEST: The standard is six feet. We've only gone five.

SMITH: It's almost one o'clock. We've been at this for almost an
hour and --

FX: **SHOVEL HITS WOODEN COFFIN LID**

SMITH: Hey!

FX: **SMITH TWICE HITS LID WITH SHOVEL**

SMITH: That's wood! I think it's the coffin!

WEST: What else would it be? We're not digging for buried
treasure. Now help me get this lid off. I want to see our
first specimen.

FX: **SMITH AND WEST DROP SHOVELS**

FX: **NAILS GROAN AS WEST AND SMITH PRY NAILS
FROM LID**

FX: **PRYING AND CICADAS FADE**

MUSIC: **CREEPY MUSIC LOW**

SMITH: (Narrating) Of my friend Herbert West I can speak only with
extreme terror.

FX: **LOW RUMBLE OF THUNDER**

SMITH: (Narrating) *A terror that began during our third year
at the Miskatonic University Medical School in Arkham, on
the day West made his incredible theory public to Professor
Holstein's chemistry class.

FX/MUSIC: * SMITH AND MUSIC FADE IN UNISON

FX: **A CLASS OF ANGRY YOUNG COLLEGE MEN BABBLING UP AS SMITH/MUSIC FADE**

SACKER: That's heresy, West! Worse, it's blasphemy!

WEST: Don't be an imbecile. It's merely true and that's that.

SACKER: "True"? It's not even false!

HOLSTEIN: (German accent) That's enough! All of you...quiet! Sacker, sit down!

FX: **BABBLING SUBSIDES AND MEN RETURN TO SEATS**

HOLSTEIN: You students should remember that this is an university, an institution dedicated to the free and open exchange of ideas.

SACKER: I'm sorry, sir.

WEST: Well spoken, Professor Holstein.

HOLSTEIN: An open exchange that includes Mr. Sacker's right to respectfully disagree with you, Mr. West.

SACKER: Professor, I would have been more respectful if this were strictly an academic argument, but I happen to know West is putting his ideas to the test.

WEST: Of course I am. A theory is no good if no one attempts to prove it. I am even preparing a paper on my research that I plan to submit to *Lancet* before year's end.

FX: **STUDENTS GRUMBLE OR CHUCKLE WITH DERISION**

HOLSTEIN: I said be quiet.

FX: **STUDENTS QUIET**

HOLSTEIN: Mr. West, I applaud your dedication and your enthusiasm. I wouldn't mind seeing more of your peers exhibiting those attributes. However, *Lancet* has published an exhaustive number of articles on the mechanistic nature of life.

WEST: Of course, but my research goes further. My aim is to artificially overcome death by means of operating a person's organic machinery by calculated chemical action after the failure of natural processes.

HOLSTEIN: That is also not a new theory. It dates back to the earliest search by alchemists for an elixir of life.

WEST: Of course. Alchemists such as Sir Isaac Newton. And to paraphrase Newton, I have been able to see further than my predecessors in such research because I stand on the shoulders of those giants.

SACKER: But Newton never spent his nights killing rodents and strays so he could try to bring them back to life like you do.

FX: **STUDENTS LAUGH**

WEST: That's a lie!

SACKER: How dare you? I say it's the truth!

WEST: Then you don't know what you're talking about!

FX: **STUDENTS GRUMBLE**

FX: **HOLSTEIN RAPS LECTERN**

HOLSTEIN: I will not warn you students again! Be quiet!

FX: **STUDENTS QUIET**

HOLSTEIN: So, Mr. West, you're not using animals for your research?

WEST: Certainly I am.

HOLSTEIN: Then you haven't killed any yourself?

WEST: Of course I have. Dozens.

HOLSTEIN: Then please explain. How did Mr. Sacker lie?

WEST: He said I tried to bring them back to life.

HOLSTEIN All right then, what were you trying to do?

WEST: I wasn't trying. I was succeeding.

FX: <u>ANGRY VOICES OF STUDENTS RISE AND OUT</u>

MUSIC: <u>DRAMATIC TRANSITION MUSIC</u>

FX: <u>WEST AND SMITH WALK ON SIDEWALK</u>

FX: <u>CHIRPING CRICKETS UNDER</u>

WEST: Sacker's an ignoramus. And Holstein isn't much better.

SMITH: Herbert, keep this up and you're going to be expelled. Then where will you be?

WEST: But no one believed me!

SMITH: I did.

WEST: Fine. You believe me. Huston Smith believes me. One person out of an entire university. I was told institutions of higher learning were bastions of intelligence and enlightenment. Except for you all I find is cynicism and intolerance. I could just as well be living in the dark ages.

SMITH: Don't sell Miskatonic short. And this is 1903. Until a generation ago, if you insisted you had brought anything back to life you would have been arrested or worse.

WEST: (Appeased) I suppose that is something. Yes. I can take some small comfort in the fact that I am traveling the same trail of persecution blazed by fellow blasphemers like Galileo and Haeckel.

SMITH: Well, I don't know if I'd say that.

WEST: Then I will. And Haeckel was right. He has to be right. Life is a chemical and physical process. The so-called soul is a myth. Add it all up and it means artificial reanimation of the dead depends only on the condition of the tissues.

FX: <u>FOOTSTEPS STOP</u>

WEST: It's a lovely moon.

SMITH: (Pleasantly surprised) Where did that come from?

WEST: Are you blind? Just look at the way the moonlight lights up
            the potter's field.

SMITH: (Realization) Oh. I see.

WEST: The grounds are so white…they look like a snow hill in the air. If I
            believed in such things I'd call this a sign.

SMITH: What sort of sign?

WEST: Of the obvious staring me in the face. I realize that the physical or
            intellectual life of a reanimated corpse might be impaired by the slight
            deterioration of the sensitive brain-cells that even a short period of
            death will cause. It's for that reason my first hope years ago was to find
            a reagent to restore vitality before the actual advent of death.

FX: SMITH TAKES A FEW STEPS CLOSER TO WEST

SMITH: Really? That sounds fascinating. What made you change your mind?

WEST: (Irresolute) To be honest, my present course didn't dawn upon
            me…until…

SMITH: Herbert? What's wrong?

WEST: (Determined) Nothing. What's past is past. But one day I am going to
            prove even Death is not immune to human retribution.

SMITH: (Intrigued) How do you plan on doing that?

WEST: If I've learned nothing else from my experiments it is that natural and
            artificial life-motions are incompatible. That's the only explanation for
            my repeated failures with animals even though I have strived for
            extreme freshness in my specimens, injecting my solutions into the
            blood immediately after death.

SMITH: What do you mean "failures"? You told Holstein's class you succeeded.

WEST: Of course I succeeded. I've obtained signs of life in dead animals
            several times, but in most cases these were violent signs. As a scientist
            how else can I rank these but failures? (To himself) *I can see now that
            perfecting my process will require a lifetime of research which must
            evolve…to the next logical stage of experimentation.

**FX: * AS WEST SPEAKS CRICKETS FADE AND CICADA WHINE
            UP**

WEST: (Quietly) Yes. Yes. The moonlight on that potter's field…is really quite…inspirational.

FX: **CICADAS OUT**

MUSIC: **LOW AND EERIE TRANSITIONAL MUSIC**

WEST: (Shocked) Dean Halsey! No! You can't!

HALSEY: Calm down, Mr. West. This isn't an expulsion. You are merely being debarred from conducting any further private experiments.

WEST: My research is at a critical fork, one I only realized last night.

HALSEY: Yes. Professor Holstein warned me about your enthusiasm. He admires it, but too much passion can lead good intentions astray without warning. I have seen enthusiasm change the course of an experiment into blind ambition many times.

WEST: That isn't the case with me. Did Professor Holstein give you my preliminary draft for a paper I'm submitting to *Lancet*?

HALSEY: Yes.

FX: **PAPERS RUSTLE**

HALSEY: I have it right here. It makes intriguing reading and demonstrates a keen mind.

WEST: If you've read it then you know my solutions have never worked the same way on different organic species but --

HALSEY: (Sadly) Your solutions never worked. Period.

FX: **WEST GASPS AS IF SLAPPED**

HALSEY: You were prudent to use the freshest specimens, considering the results your research appeared to be generating.

WEST: "Appeared"?

HALSEY: Unfortunately, in your zealousness for freshness, you failed to totally euthanize your specimens.

FX: **WEST PAUSES**

WEST: You're wrong, Dean Halsey.

HALSEY: (Startled) It's the only explanation, considering the circumstances.

WEST: (Insulted) Do you really think a third-year medical student with a "keen mind" wouldn't know how to do something as basic as take a pulse?

HALSEY: Mind your position, Mr. West. My decision is final. You will cease your experiments in reanimation.

WEST: I won't. You'll see, Dean Halsey. I'm right and --

HALSEY: (Interrupts) Enough, Mr. West. That's quite enough. I said my decision is final, and believe me, if I ever find out you are continuing your experiments I will not be so forgiving next time.

FX: **TRANSITION PAUSE**

FX: **WIND BLOWS**

FX: **CRICKETS CHIRP**

FX: **CREAKY DOOR OPENS AND SHUTS**

FX: **CRICKETS OUT**

FX: **WEST AND SMITH'S VOICES AND FOOTSTEPS ECHO IN EMPTY HOUSE**

WEST: Here we are, Huston: the Chapman farmhouse. It's been deserted since the Hayes administration, and some say the place is haunted. (Chuckles) That's rather ironic when you think about it.

FX: **FOOTSTEPS STOP**

SMITH: Why is it ironic? What are we doing here?

WEST: Please don't tell me you're that thick. Why do you think I'd drag you all the way out past Meadow Hill at this hour?

SMITH: That's exactly what…(Realization) Oh, no. Herbert, Dean Halsey interdicted your experiments.

WEST: That doesn't mean anything here. Your precious Dean Halsey has no more authority beyond the Miskatonic campus than moldy pagan gods like Baal or Dagon do outside their domains.

SMITH: No, you're wrong. We're students. We're bound by school orders wherever we go. You have to forget this idea before it's too late.

WEST: (Wryly) I'm afraid it's already too late.

FX: **WEST WALKS A FEW STEPS AND OPENS A DOOR**

WEST: Look in there.

SMITH: What have you done?

WEST: Just look. You'll be impressed.

FX: **SMITH WALKS A FEW HESITANT STEPS**

SMITH: (Gasps) Are you mad?

WEST: Holstein says I'm "enthusiastic."

SMITH: Look at all of this equipment! At all of these chemicals! Where did you get them? (Pause) Don't tell me you stole all this from the university.

WEST: No.

FX: **SMITH SIGHS WITH RELIEF**

WEST: Not all of it.

SMITH: Herbert!

WEST: I bought some of it in Boston and stocked up the rest bit by bit since my first year. I had a hunch some stuffed shirt in the medical school might eventually condemn my experiments as "too radical." I am disappointed it turned out to be Dean Halsey.

FX: **SMITH WALKS AROUND ROOM**

SMITH: There's enough here to equip an operating room and laboratory.

WEST: We can set up the laboratory next door in the kitchen. Of course the first order is to hang dark curtains on all the windows. We don't want someone who might chance by telling folks they spotted lights in here.

FX: **SMITH STOPS WALKING**

SMITH: (Thinking out loud) Well, if someone came to check it out we could say this is a chemical laboratory and...(Realization) I can't believe I said that.

WEST: I knew it! You are on my side!

FX: **WEST WALKS UP TO SMITH**

WEST: Things have changed, Huston. I can't do this alone any more.

SMITH: Wait. Wait. I thought your experiments were failures. That most of your results were violent.

WEST: Yes, and there's one more thing. My solutions never work the same way on different species.

SMITH: (Weighing information in his mind) Then that's it. There's nothing more you can do.

WEST: Of course there's more. If further animal research is pointless, that means it is time for the next logical step. My experiments must graduate to the species that it was always intended.

SMITH: (Slowly) H-e-r-b-e-r-t?

WEST: Now don't be a hypocrite. Miskatonic has never been choosey about where it gets its anatomy specimens whenever the morgue is running low. You've seen those two men who --

SMITH: Yes. I've seen them. All the medical students have.

WEST: Well, whatever two yokels can do, two brilliant medical students can, too. Especially on nights like tonight...when the moon is full...and bright...and inspirational.

SMITH: (Slowly) H-e-r-b-e-r-t?

WEST: Christchurch Cemetery is closer, which would be more convenient, but most of the bodies buried there are embalmed. That's not good for us. No, I'm afraid our pickings will have to come from the potter's field.

MUSIC: **CREEPY TRANSITION UP AND UNDER**

SMITH: (Narrating) It took a few nights to set up our new haunt, then we kept an eye on the obituaries. We were looking for particular qualifications in our specimens, specifically corpses interred soon after death and without artificial preservation. They also had to be free from malforming disease and have all their organs present. Accident victims were our best hope. A couple of months passed, though, and it started to look like we might have to stay in Arkham during the summer. Then our luck changed one day when we heard about a brawny young traveling workman named Richard Posner who had drowned the morning before in Sumner's Pond. Posner had been buried at the town's expense without delay or embalming in the potter's field.

FX: **BIRD'S CHIRP UP AND UNDER**

WEST: I found him. Over here, Huston.

FX: **SMITH'S VOICE APPROACHES AS HE TALKS**

SMITH: Where?

WEST: That marker there.

SMITH: (Reading) "Richard Posner." Yes, that's him all right.

FX: **BIRDS CHIRP UP AND UNDER AGAIN**

SMITH: It's such a sunny day. Hard to believe what we're planning to do is real. Any of it.

WEST: Don't worry about it. Once night falls and the moon is shining again, you'll be back in the right frame of mind. Now let's go get some rest. I want to begin work soon after midnight.

FX: **BIRDS CHIRP FADE**

FX: **WIND BLOWS**

FX: **CICADAS WHINE**

FX: **NAILS CREEK AND GROAN AS WEST AND SMITH PRY THEM OUT OF COFFIN'S WOODEN LID**

SMITH: That was the last nail.

WEST: (Excited) Get up on the ground and hold the oil lantern over me so I can see what I'm doing.

SMITH: Just a moment.

FX: **SMITH GRUNTS AND SCUFFLES OUT OF GRAVE**

FX: **HANDLE SQUEAKS AS LANTERN SWAYS**

WEST: Hold that light steady!

SMITH: Don't blame me. It's the wind.

WEST: Whatever it is, hold that light steady so I can see!

FX: **WEST GROANS AS HE LIFTS COFFIN LID**

WEST: All right, watch out for the lid.

FX: **WOODEN LID IS TOSSED UP ON GROUND**

WEST: Now come back here and hold the lamp over us! Hurry!

FX: **LANTERN HANDLE SQUEAKS**

FX: **NO ONE SPEAKS FOR A FEW SECONDS**

SMITH: (Uneasy) Good Lord.

WEST: (Nervous) What's the matter? You've seen dead men before.

SMITH: On dissecting-tables. In the morgue. Never in a grave. (Pause) He's so stiff. And his face. It's so vacant.

WEST: Also nothing you haven't seen before.

SMITH: (Losing his nerve) We shouldn't be here, Herbert. This isn't right.

WEST: (Slighted) Fine. Go if you want. I don't need your help.

FX: **WEST GRUNTS AS HE TRIES LIFTING CORPSE**

SMITH: You can't be serious. You'll never get him out of there by
            yourself. Even if you do, you'll never be able to lug him to
            the farmhouse alone.

WEST: I will if I have to. So go on. Do whatever it is your precious
            morals or conscience are telling you to do.

FX: **WEST GRUNTS TRYING TO LIFT CORPSE OUT OF GRAVE**

SMITH: You're being childish.

FX: **WEST GRUNTS AND STRUGGLES MORE**

SMITH: I honestly think if I left they'd find you in the morning still trying
            to get him out of there.

FX: **WEST GOES ON GRUNTING AND STRUGGLING**

SMITH: (Resigned) Fine. Make some room.

FX: **SMITH CLAMBERS INTO GRAVE**

SMITH: I'll grab him under the arms. You grab his legs. (Grunts) All
            right. I've got him. Ready? On three. One…two…

MUSIC: **TRANSITION MUSIC UP AND UNDER**

SMITH   (Narrating) We packed our specimen into a canvas bag, replaced
            the lid on the coffin, then filled in the grave. After we removed
            all trace of our visit we returned to the old Chapman place. A
            few minutes before three o'clock we laid our specimen on our
            improvised dissecting-table. West spent several minutes eying
            his prize by the light of a powerful acetylene lamp.

WEST: He appears to be a sturdy and apparently unimaginative youth of
            a wholesome common type. Large framed. Gray eyes. Brown
            hair. A sound animal, I'd say, without psychological subtleties.
            Virtually made to order for us.

MUSIC: **TRANSITION MUSIC OUT**

SMITH: "Made to order." Now that is ironic.

WEST: "Ironic"? Don't tell me you think fate had anything to do
            with this. Or could you be worried about something else?
            The so-called soul of man maybe?

SMITH: Touché. You can't tell me that you haven't thought about the secrets someone returning from the dead could tell us.

WEST: I can because I haven't.

SMITH: Really? What happened to proving even Death is not immune to human retribution?

WEST: Touché. (Pause) Of course I was speaking purely metaphorically.

SMITH: (Sarcastic) Of course.

WEST: Think what you want, Huston, but hand me that scalpel. (Pause) Thank you. Now…I'll just take his arm…and make a small incision. (Pause) That's got it. He has nice veins, I must say. Huston, hand me that vial of solution.

FX: **SMITH PICKS UP GLASS VIAL AND PULLS OUT CORK**

SMITH: Here. (Snorts) Evil smelling stuff. Worse than ammonia.

WEST: Almost bad enough to wake the dead on its own, but you get used to it. (Pause) There. Take this vial back then hand me a needle and thread so I can bind this incision.

MUSIC: **LOW EERIE MUSIC UNDER**

SMITH   (Narrating) After that, we waited. We knew there was very little chance for anything like complete success, so I could not help worrying about the possible grotesque results of partial animation. Memories and possibilities are ever more hideous than realities. West, on the other hand, never faltered. Over and over he applied his stethoscope to the specimen and each time bore the negative results philosophically. Finally, after about three quarters of an hour --

MUSIC: **LOW EERIE MUSIC FADES**

WEST: Nothing.

SMITH: (Anxious) That's it then. We've got the grave we dug in the cellar this morning ready. Let's bury him and go.

WEST: Don't be such a defeatist. Our specimen is still fresh enough for another attempt if we hurry and change the formula. I'll need the acetylene lamp in the laboratory. You can follow me unless you want to wait here in the dark.

SMITH: No thank you.

FX: **SMITH AND WEST WALK INTO NEXT ROOM**

WEST: Be a help and grab those bottles icing in the sink and bring them here.

SMITH: Fine. (Pause) Herbert, maybe this isn't the best time --

WEST: For what? More reconsideration?

SMITH: No. Re-examination. You told me once that you first set out to find a reagent to restore vitality before death. I think tonight is a sign that you should return to that course.

WEST: (Irritable) Why? There's no point to it.

FX: **SMITH AND WEST FAIL TO NOTICE A LOW, STRANGE INHALE -- AN EXHALE REVERSED ON TAPE -- AS POSNER STIRS IN NEXT ROOM**

FX: **CICADAS BEGIN TO WHINE UNDER**

SMITH: There's no point to this! Go back in the operating room and take another look at that body. A hard look. See how firmly it's gripped by Death.

WEST: (Defensive) I-said-there's-no-point! (Tired) I tried to find a reagent, Huston, but I failed.

FX: **SMITH AND WEST FAIL TO NOTICE AS STRANGE INHALE GROWS CLOSER AND SHUFFLING FOOTSTEPS OF BARE FEET APPROACH**

SMITH: How do you know you failed? I don't understand it, Herbert. You're convinced that this new course of research is going to require a lifetime, so why don't you think your original course wouldn't take as long? At least there you have a spark of life to rekindle. Here…good Lord…you've nothing but lifeless clay.

WEST: (Defensive again) To mold in my image?

SMITH: I never said that. I've never thought that's what this is about.

FX: **FOOTSTEPS AND STRANGE INHALE GROW CLOSER AS POSNER NEARS LABORATORY**

FX:	**CICADAS WHINE LOUDER**
WEST:	I'm grateful for that at least. I can't tell you how grateful I am. Now may we get back to work and what is that noise?
SMITH:	I thought I saw... (Terrified) The doorway! No!
FX:	**DOOR SLAMS**
FX:	**ACETYLENE LAMP TIPS OVER AND BREAKS**
FX:	**FLAMES CRACKLE UNDER BUT GRADUALLY GROW LOUDER**
WEST:	What are you doing?
SMITH:	Saving our lives!
WEST:	You're going to kill us! You slammed that door so hard you knocked the lamp over and acetylene is --
FX:	**STEADY POUNDING ON DOOR**
FX:	**INHUMAN WAILING FILTERS THROUGH DOOR**
WEST:	Let go of the door! We have to get out of here before the entire house is engulfed!
SMITH:	It's Posner! He's trying to get in! Can't you hear him pounding?
WEST:	Stop sounding like Halsey! I examined Posner and he's dead! That pounding is the backdraft building in the operating room! If we don't get out of here it's going to incinerate us when it burns through the door! (Struggling) Now...come...on!
SMITH:	(Trying to hold on to door) Stop it, Herbert! Let go! He'll get in!
WEST:	Not this time! I'm not letting Death get his grip on you!
SMITH:	What are you talking about?
FX:	**INHUMAN WAILING GROWS LOUDER**
WEST:	I...said...not...this...time!
SMITH:	Stop it! Stop!

FX: **WEST STRIKES SMITH OVER THE HEAD**

FX: **SMITH GRUNTS AND FALLS UNCONSCIOUS**

FX: **FLAMES GROW LOUDER**

FX: **WOOD SPLINTERS AS CEILING CRACKS**

FX: **TIMBERS TUMBLE**

MUSIC: **DRAMATIC TRANSITION MUSIC UP AND FADE**

FX: **BIRDS CHIRP UP AND RECEDE TO DISTANCE**

FX: **DOOR OPENS AND SHUTS**

FX: **WEST'S FOOTSTEPS ENTER ROOM**

WEST: For goodness sake, Huston, wake up. It's nearly five o'clock.

SMITH: (Waking) Hmm? Wha...what time did you say?

WEST: Take the cotton out of your ears. I said it's nearly five o'clock.

SMITH: (Still groggy) No...can't be...too bright outside.

WEST: Not five o'clock in the morning. You slept the day away. It's afternoon.

SMITH: What? Where am I?

WEST: (Cheery) On the divan in my boarding-room. I'm not surprised you don't remember coming back here. I hit you harder than I intended, but I had to get you out of that house. I'm sorry.

SMITH: No...no...you did the right thing. (Pause) You sound suspiciously cheerful.

WEST: Actually I like to think I sound suspiciously giddy.

FX: **SMITH SITS UP**

SMITH: Ow! My head! (Groans) I do remember one thing. During the fire...you said...you said you weren't going to let Death get his grip on me.

WEST: That does sound overly dramatic. My only excuse is that in the heat of the moment I fell back on your own words. The good news is that here you are: safe…sound…a tad singed…but alive.

SMITH: You also said "not this time." What did you mean by that?

FX: **A FEW SECONDS OF SILENCE**

SMITH: Herbert?

WEST: (Civilly) Huston, I once told you that what's past is past, and that is the only answer I am ever going to give on this subject. As my friend, I ask you to please respect my wishes and never bring that subject up again.

SMITH: (Sighs) All right. If that's how you want it.

WEST: That's how it's got to be.

SMITH: I suppose I owe you that much for saving my life. And I'm sorry I didn't say it before: thank you.

WEST: You're welcome. I'm sure that's more than I'll ever get from the other fellow.

SMITH: What other fellow?

WEST: The other fellow whose life I saved.

SMITH: "Other fellow"? Did something happen while I was out?

WEST: Quite a bit. I just came back from getting the evening edition of the newspaper. Here. Take a look at page seven.

FX: **WEST DROPS NEWSPAPER IN SMITH'S LAP**

SMITH: What else do you have there? What's in that sack?

WEST: I'll tell you after you look at page seven. Go on.

FX: **PAPERS RUSTLE AS SMITH TURNS TO PAGE SEVEN**

SMITH: Is there something in here about the fire? Did someone see it?

WEST: They saw the flames as far away as the old Gardner place!
When you commit arson, Huston, you don't go halfway!
Fortunately the fire destroyed every lick of evidence that
we were ever in the old Chapman farmhouse.

SMITH: Thank heavens. I can't say I was looking forward to going to jail for body-snatching. (Pause) I don't see anything in here about the fire.

WEST: That story is on page two. Keep looking.

SMITH: (To himself) Let's see…the reservoir is finally going to be built in the hollows west of town…local poet Edward Derby has returned from honeymoon with his wife Asenath…there was a case of vandalism in…in…oh no.

FX: **SMITH GASPS**

WEST: You found it.

SMITH: (Reading) "The grave of an itinerant laborer, Richard Posner, was disturbed by vandals last night." Good lord, Herbert, that's us! They found out we dug up his grave! I thought we were so careful!

WEST: We were careful. We're not the vandals.

SMITH: How do you know that?

WEST: I talked to a constable who was walking his beat near the newsstand where I bought the paper. I told him how horrible I thought vandalizing a grave was and asked if the police had any idea who did it. He said no. He also gave me no reason to think the police suspect Posner's body was in any way disturbed.

FX: **SMITH EXHALES IN RELIEF**

SMITH: So we're safe. This vandalism won't come back to haunt us.

WEST: Actually I don't think it was vandalism.

SMITH: (Nervous) Then what was it? Did the constable say something else?

WEST: He said it looked like someone had been clawing away at the dirt.

FX: **CICADAS WHINE UNDER**

WEST: (Casually) Hmm…the cicadas are out early tonight.

SMITH: Who would want to claw up Posner's grave?

WEST: Posner. Who else? My solution worked, Huston! It worked!

SMITH: (Disbelief) You said…you said Posner was dead.

WEST: He was dead the last time I examined him. You're the one
           Who saw him up and about.

SMITH: No! I heard…that strange sound. I don't know what it was.
           Maybe it was cicadas…or a stray animal. Then I saw some
           shadows moving. That could have been a stray animal, too.
           They…they do get into old farmhouses.

WEST: Yes, they do, but what I think happened is the effects of my
           solution were delayed, probably because the cadaver was not
           fresh enough. If I could have introduced the solution into
           Posner's blood immediately after death, I'm positive the results
           would have happened much faster.

SMITH: Even…even if that's true…why…why would he vandalize
           his own grave?

WEST: I told you, it wasn't vandalism. He was trying to dig his way
           back into his grave. To get back into his coffin. The delay
           between death and reanimation must have affected his brain
           and his thinking. That's why I doubt Posner is ever going to
           thank me for saving his life last night. Quite the contrary,
           actually. So I took the precaution of also buying this on my
           way home.

FX: **WEST PULLS A GUN OUT FROM BAG**

SMITH: A revolver?

WEST: It seemed wise, considering our present problem.

SMITH: What problem?

WEST: We know Posner is alive…but where is he now?

MUSIC: **EERIE MUSIC UP AND OUT**

SUPERNATURAL HORROR
IN LITERATURE

SOME INTRODUCTORY COMMENTS

Supernatural Horror in Literature first appeared in the single issue of *The Recluse* (May 1927) published by Lovecraft's friend W. Paul Cook, the proprietor of Vermont's Driftwood Press. Near the end of 1925 Cook approached Lovecraft about writing a critical survey of supernatural literature, and Lovecraft spent the next year researching and writing the first version of this long essay. Although justifiably proud of *Supernatural Horror in Literature*, Lovecraft continued to tinker with it until near the end of his life approximately nine years later. One revised version was partially reprinted in Charles D. Hornig's *The Fantasy Fan* (October 1933 to February 1935), the first and perhaps most prestigious fan magazine of and about weird fiction, but Lovecraft's final revised essay was not completely published until 1939 in Arkham House's *The Outsider and Others*.

An invaluable reading guide with some of the earliest and most insightful critiques on the works of Edgar Allan Poe and Arthur Machen, *Supernatural Horror in Literature* is also Lovecraft's manifesto on his brand of horror. Working on the essay made Lovecraft confront and codify his theories about weird fiction, which had an enormous impact on his own stories. Lovecraft created some of his finest fiction after completing the original version of *Supernatural Horror in Literature*, starting with *The Case of Charles Dexter Ward* and "The Colour out of Space" in 1927.

1. Introduction

The oldest and strongest emotion of mankind is fear, and the oldest and strongest kind of fear is fear of the unknown. These facts few psychologists will dispute, and their admitted truth must establish for all time the genuineness and dignity of the weirdly horrible tale as a literary form. Against it are discharged all the shafts of a materialistic sophistication which clings to frequently felt emotions and external events, and of a naively insipid idealism which deprecates the aesthetic motive and calls for a didactic literature to uplift the reader toward a suitable degree of smirking optimism. But in spite of all this opposition the weird tale has survived, developed, and attained remarkable heights of perfection; founded as it is on a profound and elementary principle whose appeal, if not always universal, must necessarily be poignant and permanent to minds of the requisite sensitiveness.

The appeal of the spectrally macabre is generally narrow because it demands from the reader a certain degree of imagination and a capacity for detachment from every-day life. Relatively few are free enough from the spell of the daily routine to respond to rappings from outside, and tales of ordinary feelings and events, or of common sentimental distortions of such feelings and events, will always take first place in the taste of the majority; rightly, perhaps, since of course these ordinary matters make up the greater part of human experience. But the sensitive are always with us, and sometimes a curious streak of fancy invades an obscure corner of the very hardest head; so that no amount of rationalisation, reform, or Freudian analysis can quite annul the thrill of the chimney-corner whisper or the lonely wood. There is here involved a psychological pattern or tradition as real and as deeply grounded in mental experience as any other pattern or tradition of mankind; coeval with the religious feeling and closely related to many aspects of it, and too much a part of our inmost biological heritage to lose keen potency over a very important, though not numerically great, minority of our species.

Man's first instincts and emotions formed his response to the environment in which he found himself. Definite feelings based on pleasure and pain grew up around the phenomena whose causes and effects he understood, whilst around those which he did not understand—and the universe teemed with them in the early days—were naturally woven such personifications, marvellous interpretations, and sensations of awe and fear as would be hit upon by a race having few and simple ideas and limited experience. The unknown, being likewise the unpredictable, became for our primitive forefathers a terrible and omnipotent source of boons and calamities visited upon mankind for cryptic and wholly extra-terrestrial reasons, and thus clearly belonging to spheres of existence whereof we know nothing and wherein we have no part. The phenomenon of dreaming likewise helped to build up the notion of an unreal or spiritual world; and in general, all the conditions of savage dawn-life so strongly conduced toward a feeling of the supernatural, that we need not wonder at the thoroughness with which man's very hereditary essence has become saturated with religion and superstition. That saturation must, as a matter of plain scientific fact, be regarded as virtually permanent so far as the subconscious mind and inner instincts are concerned; for though the area of the unknown has been steadily contracting for thousands of years, an infinite reservoir of mystery still engulfs most of the outer cosmos, whilst a vast residuum of powerful inherited associations clings around all the objects and processes that were once mysterious, however well they may now be explained. And more than this, there is an actual physiological fixation of the old instincts in our nervous tissue, which would make them obscurely operative even were the conscious mind to be purged of all sources of wonder.

Because we remember pain and the menace of death more vividly than pleasure, and because our feelings toward the beneficent aspects of the unknown have from the first been captured and formalised by conventional religious rituals, it has fallen to the lot of the darker and more maleficent side of cosmic mystery to figure chiefly in our popular supernatural folklore. This tendency, too, is naturally enhanced by the fact that uncertainty and danger are always closely allied; thus making any kind of an unknown world a world of peril and evil possibilities. When to this sense of fear and evil the inevitable fascination of wonder and curiosity is superadded, there is born a composite body of keen emotion and imaginative provocation whose vitality must of necessity endure as long as the human race itself. Children will always be afraid of the dark, and men with minds sensitive to hereditary impulse will always tremble at the thought of the hidden and fathomless worlds of strange life which may pulsate in the gulfs beyond the stars, or press hideously upon our own globe in unholy dimensions which only the dead and the moonstruck can glimpse.

With this foundation, no one need wonder at the existence of a literature of cosmic fear. It has always existed, and always will exist; and no better evidence of its tenacious vigour can be cited than the impulse which now and then drives writers of totally opposite leanings to try their hands at it in isolated tales, as if to discharge from their minds certain phantasmal shapes which would otherwise haunt them. Thus Dickens wrote several eerie narratives; Browning, the hideous poem "Childe Roland"; Henry James, *The Turn of the Screw;* Dr. Holmes, the subtle novel *Elsie Venner;* F. Marion Crawford, "The Upper Berth" and a number of other examples; Mrs. Charlotte Perkins Gilman, social worker, "The Yellow Wall Paper"; whilst the humourist W. W. Jacobs produced that able melodramatic bit called "The Monkey's Paw".

This type of fear-literature must not be confounded with a type externally similar but psychologically widely different; the literature of mere physical fear and the mundanely gruesome. Such writing, to be sure, has its place, as has the conventional or even whimsical or humorous ghost story where formalism or the author's knowing wink removes the true sense of the morbidly unnatural; but these things are not the literature of cosmic fear in its purest sense. The true weird tale has something more than secret murder, bloody bones, or a sheeted form clanking chains according to rule. A certain atmosphere of breathless and unexplainable dread of outer, unknown forces must be present; and there must be a hint, expressed with a seriousness and portentousness becoming its subject, of that most terrible conception of the human brain—a malign and particular suspension or defeat of those fixed laws of Nature which are our only safeguard against the assaults of chaos and the daemons of unplumbed space.

Naturally we cannot expect all weird tales to conform absolutely to any theoretical model. Creative minds are uneven, and the best of fabrics have their dull spots. Moreover, much of the choicest weird work is unconscious; appearing in memorable fragments scattered through material whose massed effect may be of a very different cast. Atmosphere is the all-important thing, for the final criterion of authenticity is not the dovetailing of a plot but the creation of a given sensation. We may say, as a general thing, that a weird story whose intent is to teach or produce a social effect, or one in which the horrors are finally explained away by natural means, is not a genuine tale of cosmic fear; but it remains a fact that such narratives often possess, in isolated sections, atmospheric touches which fulfil every condition of true supernatural horror-literature. Therefore we must judge a weird tale not by the author's intent, or by the mere mechanics of the plot; but by the emotional level which it attains at its least mundane point. If the proper sensations are excited, such a "high spot" must be admitted on its own merits as weird literature, no matter how prosaically it is later dragged down. The one test of the really weird is simply this—whether or not there be excited in the reader a profound sense of dread, and of contact with unknown spheres and powers; a subtle attitude of awed listening, as if for the beating of black wings or the scratching of outside shapes and entities on the known universe's utmost rim. And of course, the more completely and unifiedly a story conveys this atmosphere, the better it is as a work of art in the given medium.

2. The Dawn of the Horror-Tale

As may naturally be expected of a form so closely connected with primal emotion, the horror-tale is as old as human thought and speech themselves.

Cosmic terror appears as an ingredient of the earliest folklore of all races, and is crystallised in the most archaic ballads, chronicles, and sacred writings. It was, indeed, a prominent feature of the elaborate ceremonial magic, with its rituals for the evocation of daemons and spectres, which flourished from prehistoric times, and which reached its highest development in Egypt and the Semitic nations. Fragments like the Book of Enoch and the Claviculae of Solomon well illustrate the power of the weird over the ancient Eastern mind, and upon such things were based enduring systems and traditions whose echoes extend obscurely even to the present time. Touches of this transcendental fear are seen in classic literature, and there is evidence of its still greater emphasis in a ballad literature which paralleled the classic stream but vanished for lack of a written medium. The Middle Ages, steeped in fanciful darkness, gave it an enormous impulse toward expression; and East and West alike were busy preserving and amplifying the dark heritage, both of random folklore and of academically formulated magic and cabbalism, which had descended to them. Witch, werewolf, vampire, and ghoul brooded ominously on the lips of bard and grandam, and needed but little encouragement to take the final step across the boundary that divides the chanted tale or song from the formal literary composition. In the Orient, the weird tale tended to assume a gorgeous colouring and sprightliness which almost transmuted it into sheer phantasy. In the West, where the mystical Teuton had come down from his black Boreal forests and the Celt remembered strange sacrifices in Druidic groves, it assumed a terrible intensity and convincing seriousness of atmosphere which doubled the force of its half-told, half-hinted horrors.

Much of the power of Western horror-lore was undoubtedly due to the hidden but often suspected presence of a hideous cult of nocturnal worshippers whose strange customs—descended from pre-Aryan and pre-agricultural times when a squat race of Mongoloids roved over Europe with their flocks and herds—were rooted in the most revolting fertility-rites of immemorial antiquity. This secret religion, stealthily handed down amongst peasants for thousands of years despite the outward reign of the Druidic, Graeco-Roman, and Christian faiths in the regions involved, was marked by wild "Witches' Sabbaths" in lonely woods and atop distant hills on Walpurgis-Night and Hallowe'en, the traditional breeding-seasons of the goats and sheep and cattle; and became the source of vast riches of sorcery-legend, besides provoking extensive witchcraft-prosecutions of which the Salem affair forms the chief American example. Akin to it in essence, and perhaps connected with it in fact, was the frightful secret system of inverted theology or Satan-worship which produced such horrors as the famous "Black Mass"; whilst operating toward the same end we may note the activities of those whose aims were somewhat more scientific or philosophical—the astrologers, cabbalists, and alchemists of the Albertus Magnus or Raymond Lully type, with whom such rude ages invariably abound. The prevalence and depth of the mediaeval horror-spirit in Europe, intensified by the dark despair which waves of pestilence brought, may be fairly gauged by the grotesque carvings slyly introduced into much of the finest later Gothic ecclesiastical work of the time; the daemoniac gargoyles of

Notre Dame and Mont St. Michel being among the most famous specimens. And throughout the period, it must be remembered, there existed amongst educated and uneducated alike a most unquestioning faith in every form of the supernatural; from the gentlest of Christian doctrines to the most monstrous morbidities of witchcraft and black magic. It was from no empty background that the Renaissance magicians and alchemists—Nostradamus, Trithemius, Dr. John Dee, Robert Fludd, and the like—were born.

In this fertile soil were nourished types and characters of sombre myth and legend which persist in weird literature to this day, more or less disguised or altered by modern technique. Many of them were taken from the earliest oral sources, and form part of mankind's permanent heritage. The shade which appears and demands the burial of its bones, the daemon lover who comes to bear away his still living bride, the death-fiend or psychopomp riding the night-wind, the man-wolf, the sealed chamber, the deathless sorcerer—all these may be found in that curious body of mediaeval lore which the late Mr. Baring-Gould so effectively assembled in book form. Wherever the mystic Northern blood was strongest, the atmosphere of the popular tales became most intense; for in the Latin races there is a touch of basic rationality which denies to even their strangest superstitions many of the overtones of glamour so characteristic of our own forest-born and ice-fostered whisperings.

Just as all fiction first found extensive embodiment in poetry, so is it in poetry that we first encounter the permanent entry of the weird into standard literature. Most of the ancient instances, curiously enough, are in prose; as the werewolf incident in Petronius, the gruesome passages in Apuleius, the brief but celebrated letter of Pliny the Younger to Sura, and the odd compilation *On Wonderful Events* by the Emperor Hadrian's Greek freedman, Phlegon. It is in Phlegon that we first find that hideous tale of the corpse-bride, "Philinnion and Machates", later related by Proclus and in modern times forming the inspiration of Goethe's "Bride of Corinth" and Washington Irving's "German Student". But by the time the old Northern myths take literary form, and in that later time when the weird appears as a steady element in the literature of the day, we find it mostly in metrical dress; as indeed we find the greater part of the strictly imaginative writing of the Middle Ages and Renaissance. The Scandinavian Eddas and Sagas thunder with cosmic horror, and shake with the stark fear of Ymir and his shapeless spawn; whilst our own Anglo-Saxon *Beowulf* and the later Continental Nibelung tales are full of eldritch weirdness. Dante is a pioneer in the classic capture of macabre atmosphere, and in Spenser's stately stanzas will be seen more than a few touches of fantastic terror in landscape, incident, and character. Prose literature gives us Malory's *Morte d'Arthur*, in which are presented many ghastly situations taken from early ballad sources—the theft of the sword and silk from the corpse in Chapel Perilous by Sir Launcelot, the ghost of Sir Gawaine, and the tomb-fiend seen by Sir Galahad—whilst other and cruder specimens were doubtless set forth in the cheap and sensational "chapbooks" vulgarly hawked about and devoured by the ignorant. In Elizabethan drama, with its *Dr. Faustus*, the witches in *Macbeth*, the ghost in *Hamlet*, and the horrible gruesomeness of Webster, we may easily discern the strong hold of the daemoniac on the public mind; a hold intensified by the very real fear of living witchcraft, whose terrors, first wildest on the Continent, begin to echo loudly in English ears as the witch-hunting crusades of James the First gain headway. To the lurking mystical prose of the ages is added a long line of treatises on witchcraft and daemonology which aid in exciting the imagination of the reading world.

Through the seventeenth and into the eighteenth century we behold a growing mass of fugitive legendry and balladry of darksome cast; still, however, held down beneath the surface of polite and accepted literature. Chapbooks of horror and weirdness multiplied, and we glimpse the eager interest of the people through fragments like Defoe's "Apparition of Mrs. Veal", a homely tale of a dead woman's spectral visit to a distant friend, written to advertise covertly a badly selling theological disquisition on death. The upper orders of society were now losing faith in the supernatural, and indulging in a period of classic rationalism. Then, beginning with the translations of Eastern tales in Queen Anne's reign and taking definite form toward the middle of the century, comes the revival of romantic feeling—the era of new joy in Nature, and in the radiance of past times, strange scenes, bold deeds, and incredible marvels. We feel it first in the poets, whose utterances take on new qualities of wonder, strangeness, and shuddering. And finally, after the timid appearance of a few weird scenes in the novels of the day—such as Smollett's *Adventures of Ferdinand, Count Fathom*—the released instinct precipitates itself in the birth of a new school of writing; the "Gothic" school of horrible and fantastic prose fiction, long and short, whose literary posterity is destined to become so numerous, and in many cases so resplendent in artistic merit. It is, when one reflects upon it, genuinely remarkable that weird narration as a fixed and academically recognised literary form should have been so late of final birth. The impulse and atmosphere are as old as man, but the typical weird tale of standard literature is a child of the eighteenth century.

3. The Early Gothic Novel

The shadow-haunted landscapes of "Ossian," the chaotic visions of William Blake, the grotesque witch-dances in Burns's "Tam O'Shanter", the sinister daemonism of Coleridge's "Christabel" and *Ancient Mariner,* the ghostly charm of James Hogg's *Kilmeny,* and the more restrained approaches to cosmic horror in *Lamia* and many of Keats's other poems, are typical British illustrations of the advent of the weird to formal literature. Our Teutonic cousins of the Continent were equally receptive to the rising flood, and Bürger's "Wild Huntsman" and the even more famous daemon-bridegroom ballad of "Lenore"—both imitated in English by Scott, whose respect for the supernatural was always great—are only a taste of the eerie wealth which German song had commenced to provide. Thomas Moore adapted from such sources the legend of the ghoulish statue-bride (later used by Prosper Mérimée in "The Venus of Ille", and traceable back to great antiquity) which echoes so shiveringly in his ballad of "The Ring"; whilst Goethe's deathless masterpiece *Faust,* crossing from mere balladry into the classic, cosmic tragedy of the ages, may be held as the ultimate height to which this German poetic impulse arose.

But it remained for a very sprightly and worldly Englishman—none other than Horace Walpole himself—to give the growing impulse definite shape and become the actual founder of the literary horror-story as a permanent form. Fond of mediaeval romance and mystery as a dilettante's diversion, and with a quaintly imitated Gothic castle as his abode at Strawberry Hill, Walpole in 1764 published *The Castle of Otranto;* a tale of the supernatural which, though thoroughly unconvincing and mediocre in itself, was destined to exert an almost unparalleled influence on the literature of the weird. First venturing it only as a translation by one "William Marshal, Gent." from the Italian of a mythical "Onuphrio Muralto", the author later acknowledged his connexion with the book and took pleasure in its wide and instantaneous popularity—a popularity which extended to many editions, early dramatisation, and wholesale imitation both in England and in Germany.

The story—tedious, artificial, and melodramatic—is further impaired by a brisk and prosaic style whose urbane sprightliness nowhere permits the creation of a truly weird atmosphere. It tells of Manfred, an unscrupulous and usurping prince determined to found a line, who after the mysterious sudden death of his only son Conrad on the latter's bridal morn, attempts to put away his wife Hippolita and wed the lady destined for the unfortunate youth—the lad, by the way, having been crushed by the preternatural fall of a gigantic helmet in the castle courtyard. Isabella, the widowed bride, flees from this design; and encounters in subterranean crypts beneath the castle a noble young preserver, Theodore, who seems to be a peasant yet strangely resembles the old lord Alfonso who ruled the domain before Manfred's time. Shortly thereafter supernatural phenomena assail the castle in divers ways; fragments of gigantic armour being discovered here and there, a portrait walking out of its frame, a thunderclap destroying the edifice, and a colossal armoured spectre of Alfonso rising out of the ruins to ascend through parting clouds to the bosom of St. Nicholas. Theodore, having wooed Manfred's daughter Matilda and lost her through death—for she is slain by her father by mistake—is discovered to be the son of Alfonso and rightful heir to the estate. He concludes the tale by wedding Isabella and preparing to live happily ever after, whilst

Manfred—whose usurpation was the cause of his son's supernatural death and his own supernatural harassings—retires to a monastery for penitence; his saddened wife seeking asylum in a neighbouring convent.

Such is the tale; flat, stilted, and altogether devoid of the true cosmic horror which makes weird literature. Yet such was the thirst of the age for those touches of strangeness and spectral antiquity which it reflects, that it was seriously received by the soundest readers and raised in spite of its intrinsic ineptness to a pedestal of lofty importance in literary history. What it did above all else was to create a novel type of scene, puppet-characters, and incidents; which, handled to better advantage by writers more naturally adapted to weird creation, stimulated the growth of an imitative Gothic school which in turn inspired the real weavers of cosmic terror—the line of actual artists beginning with Poe. This novel dramatic paraphernalia consisted first of all of the Gothic castle, with its awesome antiquity, vast distances and ramblings, deserted or ruined wings, damp corridors, unwholesome hidden catacombs, and galaxy of ghosts and appalling legends, as a nucleus of suspense and daemoniac fright. In addition, it included the tyrannical and malevolent nobleman as villain; the saintly, long-persecuted, and generally insipid heroine who undergoes the major terrors and serves as a point of view and focus for the reader's sympathies; the valorous and immaculate hero, always of high birth but often in humble disguise; the convention of high-sounding foreign names, mostly Italian, for the characters; and the infinite array of stage properties which includes strange lights, damp trap-doors, extinguished lamps, mouldy hidden manuscripts, creaking hinges, shaking arras, and the like. All this paraphernalia reappears with amusing sameness, yet sometimes with tremendous effect, throughout the history of the Gothic novel; and is by no means extinct even today, though subtler technique now forces it to assume a less naive and obvious form. An harmonious milieu for a new school had been found, and the writing world was not slow to grasp the opportunity.

German romance at once responded to the Walpole influence, and soon became a byword for the weird and ghastly. In England one of the first imitators was the celebrated Mrs. Barbauld, then Miss Aikin, who in 1773 published an unfinished fragment called "Sir Bertrand", in which the strings of genuine terror were truly touched with no clumsy hand. A nobleman on a dark and lonely moor, attracted by a tolling bell and distant light, enters a strange and ancient turreted castle whose doors open and close and whose bluish will-o'-the-wisps lead up mysterious staircases toward dead hands and animated black statues. A coffin with a dead lady, whom Sir Bertrand kisses, is finally reached; and upon the kiss the scene dissolves to give place to a splendid apartment where the lady, restored to life, holds a banquet in honour of her rescuer. Walpole admired this tale, though he accorded less respect to an even more prominent offspring of his *Otranto*—*The Old English Baron*, by Clara Reeve, published in 1777. Truly enough, this tale lacks the real vibration to the note of outer darkness and mystery which distinguishes Mrs. Barbauld's fragment; and though less crude than Walpole's novel, and more artistically economical of horror in its possession of only one spectral figure, it is nevertheless too definitely insipid for greatness. Here again we have the virtuous heir to the castle disguised as a peasant and restored to his heritage through the ghost of his father; and here again we have a case of wide popularity leading to many editions, dramatisation, and ultimate translation into French. Miss Reeve wrote another weird novel, unfortunately unpublished and lost.

The Gothic novel was now settled as a literary form, and instances multiply bewilderingly as the eighteenth century draws toward its close. *The Recess,* written in 1785 by Mrs. Sophia Lee, has the historic element, revolving round the twin daughters of Mary, Queen of Scots; and though devoid of the supernatural, employs the Walpole scenery and mechanism with great dexterity. Five years later, and all existing lamps are paled by the rising of a fresh luminary of wholly superior order—Mrs. Ann Radcliffe (1764–1823), whose famous novels made terror and suspense a fashion, and who set new and higher standards in the domain of macabre and fear-inspiring atmosphere despite a provoking custom of destroying her own phantoms at the last through laboured mechanical explanations. To the familiar Gothic trappings of her predecessors Mrs. Radcliffe added a genuine sense of the unearthly in scene and incident which closely approached genius; every touch of setting and action contributing artistically to the impression of illimitable frightfulness which she wished to convey. A few sinister details like a track of blood on castle stairs, a groan from a distant vault, or a weird song in a nocturnal forest can with her conjure up the most powerful images of imminent horror; surpassing by far the extravagant and toilsome elaborations of others. Nor are these images in themselves any the less potent because they are explained away before the end of the novel. Mrs. Radcliffe's visual imagination was very strong, and appears as much in her delightful landscape touches—always in broad, glamorously pictorial outline, and never in close detail—as in her weird phantasies. Her prime weaknesses, aside from the habit of prosaic disillusionment, are a tendency toward erroneous geography and history and a fatal predilection for bestrewing her novels with insipid little poems, attributed to one or another of the characters.

Mrs. Radcliffe wrote six novels; *The Castles of Athlin and Dunbayne* (1789), *A Sicilian Romance* (1790), *The Romance of the Forest* (1791), *The Mysteries of Udolpho* (1794), *The Italian* (1797), and *Gaston de Blondeville,* composed in 1802 but first published posthumously in 1826. Of these *Udolpho* is by far the most famous, and may be taken as a type of the early Gothic tale at its best. It is the chronicle of Emily, a young Frenchwoman transplanted to an ancient and portentous castle in the Apennines through the death of her parents and the marriage of her aunt to the lord of the castle—the scheming nobleman Montoni. Mysterious sounds, opened doors, frightful legends, and a nameless horror in a niche behind a black veil all operate in quick succession to unnerve the heroine and her faithful attendant Annette; but finally, after the death of her aunt, she escapes with the aid of a fellow-prisoner whom she has discovered. On the way home she stops at a chateau filled with fresh horrors—the abandoned wing where the departed chatelaine dwelt, and the bed of death with the black pall—but is finally restored to security and happiness with her lover Valancourt, after the clearing-up of a secret which seemed for a time to involve her birth in mystery. Clearly, this is only the familiar material re-worked; but it is so well re-worked that *Udolpho* will always be a classic. Mrs. Radcliffe's characters are puppets, but they are less markedly so than those of her forerunners. And in atmospheric creation she stands preëminent among those of her time.

Of Mrs. Radcliffe's countless imitators, the American novelist Charles Brockden Brown stands the closest in spirit and method. Like her, he injured his creations by natural explanations; but also like her, he had an uncanny atmospheric power which gives his horrors a frightful vitality as long as they remain unexplained. He differed from her in contemptuously discarding the external Gothic paraphernalia and properties and choosing modern American scenes for his mysteries; but this repudiation did not extend to the Gothic spirit and type of incident. Brown's novels involve some memorably frightful scenes, and excel even Mrs. Radcliffe's in describing the operations of the perturbed mind. *Edgar Huntly* starts with a sleep-walker digging a grave, but is later impaired by touches of Godwinian didacticism. *Ormond* involves a member of a sinister secret brotherhood. That and *Arthur Mervyn* both describe the plague of yellow fever, which the author had witnessed in Philadelphia and New York. But Brown's most famous book is *Wieland; or, The Transformation* (1798), in which a Pennsylvania German, engulfed by a wave of religious fanaticism, hears voices and slays his wife and children as a sacrifice. His sister Clara, who tells the story, narrowly escapes. The scene, laid at the woodland estate of Mittingen on the Schuylkill's remote reaches, is drawn with extreme vividness; and the terrors of Clara, beset by spectral tones, gathering fears, and the sound of strange footsteps in the lonely house, are all shaped with truly artistic force. In the end a lame ventriloquial explanation is offered, but the atmosphere is genuine while it lasts. Carwin, the malign ventriloquist, is a typical villain of the Manfred or Montoni type.

4. The Apex of Gothic Romance

Horror in literature attains a new malignity in the work of Matthew Gregory Lewis (1775–1818), whose novel *The Monk* (1796) achieved marvellous popularity and earned him the nickname of "Monk" Lewis. This young author, educated in Germany and saturated with a body of wild Teuton lore unknown to Mrs. Radcliffe, turned to terror in forms more violent than his gentle predecessor had ever dared to think of; and produced as a result a masterpiece of active nightmare whose general Gothic cast is spiced with added stores of ghoulishness. The story is one of a Spanish monk, Ambrosio, who from a state of overproud virtue is tempted to the very nadir of evil by a fiend in the guise of the maiden Matilda; and who is finally, when awaiting death at the Inquisition's hands, induced to purchase escape at the price of his soul from the Devil, because he deems both body and soul already lost. Forthwith the mocking Fiend snatches him to a lonely place, tells him he has sold his soul in vain since both pardon and a chance for salvation were approaching at the moment of his hideous bargain, and completes the sardonic betrayal by rebuking him for his unnatural crimes, and casting his body down a precipice whilst his soul is borne off for ever to perdition. The novel contains some appalling descriptions such as the incantation in the vaults beneath the convent cemetery, the burning of the convent, and the final end of the wretched abbot. In the sub-plot where the Marquis de las Cisternas meets the spectre of his erring ancestress, The Bleeding Nun, there are many enormously potent strokes; notably the visit of the animated corpse to the Marquis's bedside, and the cabbalistic ritual whereby the Wandering Jew helps him to fathom and banish his dead tormentor. Nevertheless *The Monk* drags sadly when read as a whole. It is too long and too diffuse, and much of its potency is marred by flippancy and by an awkwardly excessive reaction against those canons of decorum which Lewis at first despised as prudish. One great thing may be said of the author; that he never ruined his ghostly visions with a natural explanation. He succeeded in breaking up the Radcliffian tradition and expanding the field of the Gothic novel. Lewis wrote much more than *The Monk*. His drama, *The Castle Spectre*, was produced in 1798, and he later found time to pen other fictions in ballad form— *Tales of Terror* (1799), *Tales of Wonder* (1801), and a succession of translations from the German.

Gothic romances, both English and German, now appeared in multitudinous and mediocre profusion. Most of them were merely ridiculous in the light of mature taste, and Miss Austen's famous satire *Northanger Abbey* was by no means an unmerited rebuke to a school which had sunk far toward absurdity. This particular school was petering out, but before its final subordination there arose its last and greatest figure in the person of Charles Robert Maturin (1782–1824), an obscure and eccentric Irish clergyman. Out of an ample body of miscellaneous writing which includes one confused Radcliffian imitation called *Fatal Revenge; or, The Family of Montorio* (1807), Maturin at length evolved the vivid horror-masterpiece of *Melmoth the Wanderer* (1820), in which the Gothic tale climbed to altitudes of sheer spiritual fright which it had never known before.

Melmoth is the tale of an Irish gentleman who, in the seventeenth century, obtained a preternaturally extended life from the Devil at the price of his soul. If he can persuade another to take the bargain off his hands, and assume his existing state, he can be saved; but this he can never manage to effect, no matter how assiduously he haunts those whom despair has made reckless and frantic. The framework of the story is very clumsy; involving tedious length, digressive episodes, narratives within narratives, and laboured dovetailing and coincidences; but at various points in the endless rambling there is felt a pulse of power undiscoverable in any previous work of this kind—a kinship to the essential truth of human nature, an understanding of the profoundest sources of actual cosmic fear, and a white heat of sympathetic passion on the writer's part which makes the book a true document of aesthetic self-expression rather than a mere clever compound of artifice. No unbiassed reader can doubt that with *Melmoth* an enormous stride in the evolution of the horror-tale is represented. Fear is taken out of the realm of the conventional and exalted into a hideous cloud over mankind's very destiny. Maturin's shudders, the work of one capable of shuddering himself, are of the sort that convince. Mrs. Radcliffe and Lewis are fair game for the parodist, but it would be difficult to find a false note in the feverishly intensified action and high atmospheric tension of the Irishman whose less sophisticated emotions and strain of Celtic mysticism gave him the finest possible natural equipment for his task. Without a doubt Maturin is a man of authentic genius, and he was so recognised by Balzac, who grouped Melmoth with Molière's Don Juan, Goethe's Faust, and Byron's Manfred as the supreme allegorical figures of modern European literature, and wrote a whimsical piece called "Melmoth Reconciled", in which the Wanderer succeeds in passing his infernal bargain on to a Parisian bank defaulter, who in turn hands it along a chain of victims until a revelling gambler dies with it in his possession, and by his damnation ends the curse. Scott, Rossetti, Thackeray, and Baudelaire are the other titans who gave Maturin their unqualified admiration, and there is much significance in the fact that Oscar Wilde, after his disgrace and exile, chose for his last days in Paris the assumed name of "Sebastian Melmoth".

Melmoth contains scenes which even now have not lost their power to evoke dread. It begins with a deathbed—an old miser is dying of sheer fright because of something he has seen, coupled with a manuscript he has read and a family portrait which hangs in an obscure closet of his centuried home in County Wicklow. He sends to Trinity College, Dublin, for his nephew John; and the latter upon arriving notes many uncanny things. The eyes of the portrait in the closet glow horribly, and twice a figure strangely resembling the portrait appears momentarily at the door. Dread hangs over that house of the Melmoths, one of whose ancestors, "J. Melmoth, 1646", the portrait represents. The dying miser declares that this man—at a date slightly before 1800—is alive. Finally the miser dies, and the nephew is told in the will to destroy both the portrait and a manuscript to be found in a certain drawer. Reading the manuscript, which was written late in the seventeenth century by an Englishman named Stanton, young John learns of a terrible incident in Spain in 1677, when the writer met a horrible fellow-countryman and was told of how he had stared to death a priest who tried to denounce him as one filled with fearsome evil. Later, after meeting the man again in London, Stanton is cast into a madhouse and visited by the stranger, whose approach is heralded by spectral music and whose eyes have a more than mortal glare. Melmoth the Wanderer—for such is the malign visitor—offers the captive freedom if he will take over his bargain with the Devil; but like all others whom Melmoth has approached, Stanton is proof against temptation. Melmoth's description of the horrors of a life in a madhouse, used to tempt Stanton, is one of the most potent passages of the book. Stanton is at length liberated, and spends the rest of his life tracking down Melmoth, whose family and ancestral abode he discovers. With the family he leaves the manuscript, which by young John's time is sadly ruinous and fragmentary. John destroys both portrait and manuscript, but in sleep is visited by his horrible ancestor, who leaves a black and blue mark on his wrist.

Young John soon afterward receives as a visitor a shipwrecked Spaniard, Alonzo de Monçada, who has escaped from compulsory monasticism and from the perils of the Inquisition. He has suffered horribly—and the descriptions of his experiences under torment and in the vaults through which he once essays escape are classic—but had the strength to resist Melmoth the Wanderer when approached at his darkest hour in prison. At the house of a Jew who sheltered him after his escape he discovers a wealth of manuscript relating other exploits of Melmoth including his wooing of an Indian island maiden, Immalee, who later comes to her birthright in Spain and is known as Donna Isidora; and of his horrible marriage to her by the corpse of a dead anchorite at midnight in the ruined chapel of a shunned and abhorred monastery. Monçada's narrative to young John takes up the bulk of Maturin's four-volume book; this disproportion being considered one of the chief technical faults of the composition.

At last the colloquies of John and Monçada are interrupted by the entrance of Melmoth the Wanderer himself, his piercing eyes now fading, and decrepitude swiftly overtaking him. The term of his bargain has approached its end, and he has come home after a century and a half to meet his fate. Warning all others from the room, no matter what sounds they may hear in the night, he awaits the end alone. Young John and Monçada hear frightful ululations, but do not intrude till silence comes toward morning. They then find the room empty. Clayey footprints lead out a rear door to a cliff overlooking the sea, and near the edge of the precipice is a track indicating the forcible dragging of some heavy body. The Wanderer's scarf is found on a crag some distance below the brink, but nothing further is ever seen or heard of him.

Such is the story, and none can fail to notice the difference between this modulated, suggestive, and artistically moulded horror and—to use the words of Professor George Saintsbury—"the artful but rather jejune rationalism of Mrs. Radcliffe, and the too often puerile extravagance, the bad taste, and the sometimes slipshod style of Lewis." Maturin's style in itself deserves particular praise, for its forcible directness and vitality lift it altogether above the pompous artificialities of which his predecessors are guilty. Professor Edith Birkhead, in her history of the Gothic novel, justly observes that with all his faults Maturin was the greatest as well as the last of the Goths. *Melmoth* was widely read and eventually dramatised, but its late date in the evolution of the Gothic tale deprived it of the tumultuous popularity of *Udolpho* and *The Monk*.

5. The Aftermath of Gothic Fiction

Meanwhile other hands had not been idle, so that above the dreary plethora of trash like Marquis von Grosse's *Horrid Mysteries* (1796), Mrs. Roche's *Children of the Abbey* (1796), Miss Dacre's *Zofloya; or, The Moor* (1806), and the poet Shelley's schoolboy effusions *Zastrozzi* (1810) and *St. Irvyne* (1811) (both imitations of *Zofloya*) there arose many memorable weird works both in English and German. Classic in merit, and markedly different from its fellows because of its foundation in the Oriental tale rather than the Walpolesque Gothic novel, is the celebrated *History of the Caliph Vathek* by the wealthy dilettante William Beckford, first written in the French language but published in an English translation before the appearance of the original. Eastern tales, introduced to European literature early in the eighteenth century through Galland's French translation of the inexhaustibly opulent *Arabian Nights,* had become a reigning fashion; being used both for allegory and for amusement. The sly humour which only the Eastern mind knows how to mix with weirdness had captivated a sophisticated generation, till Bagdad and Damascus names became as freely strown through popular literature as dashing Italian and Spanish ones were soon to be. Beckford, well read in Eastern romance, caught the atmosphere with unusual receptivity; and in his fantastic volume reflected very potently the haughty luxury, sly disillusion, bland cruelty, urbane treachery, and shadowy spectral horror of the Saracen spirit. His seasoning of the ridiculous seldom mars the force of his sinister theme, and the tale marches onward with a phantasmagoric pomp in which the laughter is that of skeletons feasting under Arabesque domes. *Vathek* is a tale of the grandson of the Caliph Haroun, who, tormented by that ambition for super-terrestrial power, pleasure, and learning which animates the average Gothic villain or Byronic hero (essentially cognate types), is lured by an evil genius to seek the subterranean throne of the mighty and fabulous pre-Adamite sultans in the fiery halls of Eblis, the Mahometan Devil. The descriptions of Vathek's palaces and diversions, of his scheming sorceress-mother Carathis and her witch-tower with the fifty one-eyed negresses, of his pilgrimage to the haunted ruins of Istakhar (Persepolis) and of the impish bride Nouronihar whom he treacherously acquired on the way, of Istakhar's primordial towers and terraces in the burning moonlight of the waste, and of the terrible Cyclopean halls of Eblis, where, lured by glittering promises, each victim is compelled to wander in anguish for ever, his right hand upon his blazingly ignited and eternally burning heart, are triumphs of weird colouring which raise the book to a permanent place in English letters. No less notable are the three *Episodes of Vathek,* intended for insertion in the tale as narratives of Vathek's fellow-victims in Eblis' infernal halls, which remained unpublished throughout the author's lifetime and were discovered as recently as 1909 by the scholar Lewis Melville whilst collecting material for his *Life and Letters of William Beckford.* Beckford, however, lacks the essential mysticism which marks the acutest form of the weird; so that his tales have a certain knowing Latin hardness and clearness preclusive of sheer panic fright.

But Beckford remained alone in his devotion to the Orient. Other writers, closer to the Gothic tradition and to European life in general, were content to follow more faithfully in the lead of Walpole. Among the countless producers of terror-literature in these times may be mentioned the Utopian economic theorist William Godwin, who followed his famous but non-supernatural *Caleb Williams* (1794) with the intendedly weird *St. Leon* (1799), in which the theme of the elixir of life, as developed by the imaginary secret order of "Rosicrucians", is handled with ingeniousness if not with atmospheric convincingness. This element of Rosicrucianism, fostered by a wave of popular magical interest exemplified in the vogue of the charlatan Cagliostro and the publication of Francis Barrett's *The Magus* (1801), a curious and compendious treatise on occult principles and ceremonies, of which a reprint was made as lately as 1896, figures in Bulwer-Lytton and in many late Gothic novels, especially that remote and enfeebled posterity which straggled far down into the nineteenth century and was represented by George W. M. Reynolds' *Faust and the Demon* and *Wagner, the Wehr-wolf*. *Caleb Williams*, though non-supernatural, has many authentic touches of terror. It is the tale of a servant persecuted by a master whom he has found guilty of murder, and displays an invention and skill which have kept it alive in a fashion to this day. It was dramatised as *The Iron Chest*, and in that form was almost equally celebrated. Godwin, however, was too much the conscious teacher and prosaic man of thought to create a genuine weird masterpiece.

His daughter, the wife of Shelley, was much more successful; and her inimitable *Frankenstein; or, The Modern Prometheus* (1818) is one of the horror-classics of all time. Composed in competition with her husband, Lord Byron, and Dr. John William Polidori in an effort to prove supremacy in horror-making, Mrs. Shelley's *Frankenstein* was the only one of the rival narratives to be brought to an elaborate completion; and criticism has failed to prove that the best parts are due to Shelley rather than to her. The novel, somewhat tinged but scarcely marred by moral didacticism, tells of the artificial human being moulded from charnel fragments by Victor Frankenstein, a young Swiss medical student. Created by its designer "in the mad pride of intellectuality", the monster possesses full intelligence but owns a hideously loathsome form. It is rejected by mankind, becomes embittered, and at length begins the successive murder of all whom young Frankenstein loves best, friends and family. It demands that Frankenstein create a wife for it; and when the student finally refuses in horror lest the world be populated with such monsters, it departs with a hideous threat 'to be with him on his wedding night'. Upon that night the bride is strangled, and from that time on Frankenstein hunts down the monster, even into the wastes of the Arctic. In the end, whilst seeking shelter on the ship of the man who tells the story, Frankenstein himself is killed by the shocking object of his search and creation of his presumptuous pride. Some of the scenes in *Frankenstein* are unforgettable, as when the newly animated monster enters its creator's room, parts the curtains of his bed, and gazes at him in the yellow moonlight with watery eyes—"if eyes they may be called". Mrs. Shelley wrote other novels, including the fairly notable *Last Man;* but never duplicated the success of her first effort. It has the true touch of cosmic fear, no matter how much the movement may lag in places. Dr. Polidori developed his competing idea as a long short story, "The Vampyre"; in which we behold a suave villain of the true Gothic or Byronic type, and encounter some excellent passages of stark fright, including a terrible nocturnal experience in a shunned Grecian wood.

In this same period Sir Walter Scott frequently concerned himself with the weird, weaving it into many of his novels and poems, and sometimes producing such independent bits of narration as "The Tapestried Chamber" or "Wandering Willie's Tale" in *Redgauntlet,* in the latter of which the force of the spectral and the diabolic is enhanced by a grotesque homeliness of speech and atmosphere. In 1830 Scott published his *Letters on Demonology and Witchcraft,* which still forms one of our best compendia of European witch-lore. Washington Irving is another famous figure not unconnected with the weird; for though most of his ghosts are too whimsical and humorous to form genuinely spectral literature, a distinct inclination in this direction is to be noted in many of his productions. "The German Student" in *Tales of a Traveller* (1824) is a slyly concise and effective presentation of the old legend of the dead bride, whilst woven into the comic tissue of "The Money-Diggers" in the same volume is more than one hint of piratical apparitions in the realms which Captain Kidd once roamed. Thomas Moore also joined the ranks of the macabre artists in the poem *Alciphron,* which he later elaborated into the prose novel of *The Epicurean* (1827). Though merely relating the adventures of a young Athenian duped by the artifice of cunning Egyptian priests, Moore manages to infuse much genuine horror into his account of subterranean frights and wonders beneath the primordial temples of Memphis. De Quincey more than once revels in grotesque and arabesque terrors, though with a desultoriness and learned pomp which deny him the rank of specialist.

This era likewise saw the rise of William Harrison Ainsworth, whose romantic novels teem with the eerie and the gruesome. Capt. Marryat, besides writing such short tales as "The Werewolf", made a memorable contribution in *The Phantom Ship* (1839), founded on the legend of the Flying Dutchman, whose spectral and accursed vessel sails for ever near the Cape of Good Hope. Dickens now rises with occasional weird bits like "The Signalman", a tale of ghostly warning conforming to a very common pattern and touched with a verisimilitude which allies it as much with the coming psychological school as with the dying Gothic school. At this time a wave of interest in spiritualistic charlatanry, mediumism, Hindoo theosophy, and such matters, much like that of the present day, was flourishing; so that the number of weird tales with a "psychic" or pseudo-scientific basis became very considerable. For a number of these the prolific and popular Lord Edward Bulwer-Lytton was responsible; and despite the large doses of turgid rhetoric and empty romanticism in his products, his success in the weaving of a certain kind of bizarre charm cannot be denied.

"The House and the Brain", which hints of Rosicrucianism and at a malign and deathless figure perhaps suggested by Louis XV's mysterious courtier St. Germain, yet survives as one of the best short haunted-house tales ever written. The novel *Zanoni* (1842) contains similar elements more elaborately handled, and introduces a vast unknown sphere of being pressing on our own world and guarded by a horrible "Dweller of the Threshold" who haunts those who try to enter and fail. Here we have a benign brotherhood kept alive from age to age till finally reduced to a single member, and as a hero an ancient Chaldaean sorcerer surviving in the pristine bloom of youth to perish on the guillotine of the French Revolution. Though full of the conventional spirit of romance, marred by a ponderous network of symbolic and didactic meanings, and left unconvincing through lack of perfect atmospheric realisation of the situations hinging on the spectral world, *Zanoni* is really an excellent performance as a romantic novel; and can be read with genuine interest today by the not too sophisticated reader. It is amusing to note that in describing an attempted initiation into the ancient brotherhood the author cannot escape using the stock Gothic castle of Walpolian lineage.

In *A Strange Story* (1862) Bulwer-Lytton shews a marked improvement in the creation of weird images and moods. The novel, despite enormous length, a highly artificial plot bolstered up by opportune coincidences, and an atmosphere of homiletic pseudo-science designed to please the matter-of-fact and purposeful Victorian reader, is exceedingly effective as a narrative; evoking instantaneous and unflagging interest, and furnishing many potent—if somewhat melodramatic—tableaux and climaxes. Again we have the mysterious user of life's elixir in the person of the soulless magician Margrave, whose dark exploits stand out with dramatic vividness against the modern background of a quiet English town and of the Australian bush; and again we have shadowy intimations of a vast spectral world of the unknown in the very air about us— this time handled with much greater power and vitality than in *Zanoni*. One of the two great incantation passages, where the hero is driven by a luminous evil spirit to rise at night in his sleep, take a strange Egyptian wand, and evoke nameless presences in the haunted and mausoleum-facing pavilion of a famous Renaissance alchemist, truly stands among the major terror scenes of literature. Just enough is suggested, and just little enough is told. Unknown words are twice dictated to the sleep-walker, and as he repeats them the ground trembles, and all the dogs of the countryside begin to bay at half-seen amorphous shadows that stalk athwart the moonlight. When a third set of unknown words is prompted, the sleep-walker's spirit suddenly rebels at uttering them, as if the soul could recognise ultimate abysmal horrors concealed from the mind; and at last an apparition of an absent sweetheart and good angel breaks the malign spell. This fragment well illustrates how far Lord Lytton was capable of progressing beyond his usual pomp and stock romance toward that crystalline essence of artistic fear which belongs to the domain of poetry. In describing certain details of incantations, Lytton was greatly indebted to his amusingly serious occult studies, in the course of which he came in touch with that odd French scholar and cabbalist Alphonse-Louis Constant ("Eliphas Lévi"), who claimed to possess the secrets of ancient magic, and to have evoked the spectre of the old Grecian wizard Apollonius of Tyana, who lived in Nero's time.

The romantic, semi-Gothic, quasi-moral tradition here represented was carried far down the nineteenth century by such authors as Joseph Sheridan Le Fanu, Thomas Preskett Prest with his famous *Varney, the Vampyre* (1847), Wilkie Collins, the late Sir H. Rider Haggard (whose *She* is really remarkably good), Sir A. Conan Doyle, H. G. Wells, and Robert Louis Stevenson—the latter of whom, despite an atrocious tendency toward jaunty mannerisms, created permanent classics in "Markheim", "The Body-Snatcher", and *Dr. Jekyll and Mr. Hyde*. Indeed, we may say that this school still survives; for to it clearly belong such of our contemporary horror-tales as specialise in events rather than atmospheric details, address the intellect rather than the impressionistic imagination, cultivate a luminous glamour rather than a malign tensity or psychological verisimilitude, and take a definite stand in sympathy with mankind and its welfare. It has its undeniable strength, and because of its "human element" commands a wider audience than does the sheer artistic nightmare. If not quite so potent as the latter, it is because a diluted product can never achieve the intensity of a concentrated essence.

Quite alone both as a novel and as a piece of terror-literature stands the famous *Wuthering Heights* (1847) by Emily Brontë, with its mad vista of bleak, windswept Yorkshire moors and the violent, distorted lives they foster. Though primarily a tale of life, and of human passions in agony and conflict, its epically cosmic setting affords room for horror of the most spiritual sort. Heathcliff, the modified Byronic villain-hero, is a strange dark waif found in the streets as a small child and speaking only a strange gibberish till adopted by the family he ultimately ruins. That he is in truth a diabolic spirit rather than a human being is more than once suggested, and the unreal is further approached in the experience of the visitor who encounters a plaintive child-ghost at a bough-brushed upper window. Between Heathcliff and Catherine Earnshaw is a tie deeper and more terrible than human love. After her death he twice disturbs her grave, and is haunted by an impalpable presence which can be nothing less than her spirit. The spirit enters his life more and more, and at last he becomes confident of some imminent mystical reunion. He says he feels a strange change approaching, and ceases to take nourishment. At night he either walks abroad or opens the casement by his bed. When he dies the casement is still swinging open to the pouring rain, and a queer smile pervades the stiffened face. They bury him in a grave beside the mound he has haunted for eighteen years, and small shepherd boys say that he yet walks with his Catherine in the churchyard and on the moor when it rains. Their faces, too, are sometimes seen on rainy nights behind that upper casement at Wuthering Heights. Miss Brontë's eerie terror is no mere Gothic echo, but a tense expression of man's shuddering reaction to the unknown. In this respect, *Wuthering Heights* becomes the symbol of a literary transition, and marks the growth of a new and sounder school.

6. Spectral Literature on the Continent

On the continent literary horror fared well. The celebrated short tales and novels of Ernst Theodor Wilhelm Hoffmann (1776–1822) are a byword for mellowness of background and maturity of form, though they incline to levity and extravagance, and lack the exalted moments of stark, breathless terror which a less sophisticated writer might have achieved. Generally they convey the grotesque rather than the terrible. Most artistic of all the Continental weird tales is the German classic *Undine* (1811), by Friedrich Heinrich Karl, Baron de la Motte Fouqué. In this story of a water-spirit who married a mortal and gained a human soul there is a delicate fineness of craftsmanship which makes it notable in any department of literature, and an easy naturalness which places it close to the genuine folk-myth. It is, in fact, derived from a tale told by the Renaissance physician and alchemist Paracelsus in his *Treatise on Elemental Sprites*.

Undine, daughter of a powerful water-prince, was exchanged by her father as a small child for a fisherman's daughter, in order that she might acquire a soul by wedding a human being. Meeting the noble youth Huldbrand at the cottage of her foster-father by the sea at the edge of a haunted wood, she soon marries him, and accompanies him to his ancestral castle of Ringstetten. Huldbrand, however, eventually wearies of his wife's supernatural affiliations, and especially of the appearances of her uncle, the malicious woodland waterfall-spirit Kühleborn; a weariness increased by his growing affection for Bertalda, who turns out to be the fisherman's child for whom Undine was exchanged. At length, on a voyage down the Danube, he is provoked by some innocent act of his devoted wife to utter the angry words which consign her back to her supernatural element; from which she can, by the laws of her species, return only once—to kill him, whether she will or no, if ever he prove unfaithful to her memory. Later, when Huldbrand is about to be married to Bertalda, Undine returns for her sad duty, and bears his life away in tears. When he is buried among his fathers in the village churchyard a veiled, snow-white female figure appears among the mourners, but after the prayer is seen no more. In her place is seen a little silver spring, which murmurs its way almost completely around the new grave, and empties into a neighbouring lake. The villagers shew it to this day, and say that Undine and her Huldbrand are thus united in death. Many passages and atmospheric touches in this tale reveal Fouqué as an accomplished artist in the field of the macabre; especially the descriptions of the haunted wood with its gigantic snow-white man and various unnamed terrors, which occur early in the narrative.

Not so well known as *Undine,* but remarkable for its convincing realism and freedom from Gothic stock devices, is the *Amber Witch* of Wilhelm Meinhold, another product of the German fantastic genius of the earlier nineteenth century. This tale, which is laid in the time of the Thirty Years' War, purports to be a clergyman's manuscript found in an old church at Coserow, and centres round the writer's daughter, Maria Schweidler, who is wrongly accused of witchcraft. She has found a deposit of amber which she keeps secret for various reasons, and the unexplained wealth obtained from this lends colour to the accusation; an accusation instigated by the malice of the wolf-hunting nobleman Wittich Appelmann, who has vainly pursued her with ignoble designs. The deeds of a real witch, who afterward comes to a horrible supernatural end in prison, are glibly imputed to the hapless Maria; and after a typical witchcraft trial with forced confessions under torture she is about to be burned at the stake when saved just in time by her lover, a noble youth from a neighbouring district. Meinhold's great strength is in his air of casual and realistic verisimilitude, which intensifies our suspense and sense of the unseen by half persuading us that the menacing events must somehow be either the truth or very close to the truth. Indeed, so thorough is this realism that a popular magazine once published the main points of *The Amber Witch* as an actual occurrence of the seventeenth century!

In the present generation German horror-fiction is most notably represented by Hanns Heinz Ewers, who brings to bear on his dark conceptions an effective knowledge of modern psychology. Novels like *The Sorcerer's Apprentice* and *Alraüne*, and short stories like "The Spider", contain distinctive qualities which raise them to a classic level.

But France as well as Germany has been active in the realm of weirdness. Victor Hugo, in such tales as *Hans of Iceland*, and Balzac, in *The Wild Ass's Skin*, *Séraphîta*, and *Louis Lambert*, both employ supernaturalism to a greater or less extent; though generally only as a means to some more human end, and without the sincere and daemonic intensity which characterises the born artist in shadows. It is in Théophile Gautier that we first seem to find an authentic French sense of the unreal world, and here there appears a spectral mastery which, though not continuously used, is recognisable at once as something alike genuine and profound. Short tales like "Avatar", "The Foot of the Mummy", and "Clarimonde" display glimpses of forbidden visits that allure, tantalise, and sometimes horrify; whilst the Egyptian visions evoked in "One of Cleopatra's Nights" are of the keenest and most expressive potency. Gautier captured the inmost soul of aeon-weighted Egypt, with its cryptic life and Cyclopean architecture, and uttered once and for all the eternal horror of its nether world of catacombs, where to the end of time millions of stiff, spiced corpses will stare up in the blackness with glassy eyes, awaiting some awesome and unrelatable summons. Gustave Flaubert ably continued the tradition of Gautier in orgies of poetic phantasy like *The Temptation of St. Anthony*, and but for a strong realistic bias might have been an arch-weaver of tapestried terrors. Later on we see the stream divide, producing strange poets and fantaisistes of the Symbolist and Decadent schools whose dark interests really centre more in abnormalities of human thought and instinct than in the actual supernatural, and subtle story-tellers whose thrills are quite directly derived from the night-black wells of cosmic unreality. Of the former class of "artists in sin" the illustrious poet Baudelaire, influenced vastly by Poe, is the supreme type; whilst the psychological novelist Joris-Karl Huysmans, a true child of the eighteen-nineties, is at once the summation and finale. The latter and purely narrative class is continued by Prosper Mérimée, whose "Venus of Ille" presents in terse and convincing prose the same ancient statue-bride theme which Thomas Moore cast in ballad form in "The Ring".

The horror-tales of the powerful and cynical Guy de Maupassant, written as his final madness gradually overtook him, present individualities of their own; being rather the morbid outpourings of a realistic mind in a pathological state than the healthy imaginative products of a vision naturally disposed toward phantasy and sensitive to the normal illusions of the unseen. Nevertheless they are of the keenest interest and poignancy; suggesting with marvellous force the imminence of nameless terrors, and the relentless dogging of an ill-starred individual by hideous and menacing representatives of the outer blackness. Of these stories "The Horla" is generally regarded as the masterpiece. Relating the advent to France of an invisible being who lives on water and milk, sways the minds of others, and seems to be the vanguard of a horde of extra-terrestrial organisms arrived on earth to subjugate and overwhelm mankind, this tense narrative is perhaps without a peer in its particular department; notwithstanding its indebtedness to a tale by the American Fitz-James O'Brien for details in describing the actual presence of the unseen monster. Other potently dark creations of de Maupassant are "Who Knows?", "The Spectre", "He?", "The Diary of a Madman", "The White Wolf", "On the River", and the grisly verses entitled "Horror".

The collaborators Erckmann-Chatrian enriched French literature with many spectral fancies like *The Man-Wolf*, in which a transmitted curse works toward its end in a traditional Gothic-castle setting. Their power of creating a shuddering midnight atmosphere was tremendous despite a tendency toward natural explanations and scientific wonders; and few short tales contain greater horror than "The Invisible Eye", where a malignant old hag weaves nocturnal hypnotic spells which induce the successive occupants of a certain inn chamber to hang themselves on a cross-beam. "The Owl's Ear" and "The Waters of Death" are full of engulfing darkness and mystery, the latter embodying the familiar overgrown-spider theme so frequently employed by weird fictionists. Villiers de l'Isle-Adam likewise followed the macabre school; his "Torture by Hope", the tale of a stake-condemned prisoner permitted to escape in order to feel the pangs of recapture, being held by some to constitute the most harrowing short story in literature. This type, however, is less a part of the weird tradition than a class peculiar to itself—the so-called *conte cruel*, in which the wrenching of the emotions is accomplished through dramatic tantalisations, frustrations, and gruesome physical horrors. Almost wholly devoted to this form is the living writer Maurice Level, whose very brief episodes have lent themselves so readily to theatrical adaptation in the "thrillers" of the Grand Guignol. As a matter of fact, the French genius is more naturally suited to this dark realism than to the suggestion of the unseen; since the latter process requires, for its best and most sympathetic development on a large scale, the inherent mysticism of the Northern mind.

A very flourishing, though till recently quite hidden, branch of weird literature is that of the Jews, kept alive and nourished in obscurity by the sombre heritage of early Eastern magic, apocalyptic literature, and cabbalism. The Semitic mind, like the Celtic and Teutonic, seems to possess marked mystical inclinations; and the wealth of underground horror-lore surviving in ghettoes and synagogues must be much more considerable than is generally imagined. Cabbalism itself, so prominent during the Middle Ages, is a system of philosophy explaining the universe as emanations of the Deity, and involving the existence of strange spiritual realms and beings apart from the visible world, of which dark glimpses may be obtained through certain secret incantations. Its ritual is bound up with mystical interpretations of the Old Testament, and attributes an esoteric significance to each letter of the Hebrew alphabet—a circumstance which has imparted to Hebrew letters a sort of spectral glamour and potency in the popular literature of magic. Jewish folklore has preserved much of the terror and mystery of the past, and when more thoroughly studied is likely to exert considerable influence on weird fiction. The best examples of its literary use so far are the German novel *The Golem*, by Gustav Meyrink, and the drama *The Dybbuk*, by the

Jewish writer using the pseudonym "Ansky". The former, with its haunting shadowy suggestions of marvels and horrors just beyond reach, is laid in Prague, and describes with singular mastery that city's ancient ghetto with its spectral, peaked gables. The name is derived from a fabulous artificial giant supposed to be made and animated by mediaeval rabbis according to a certain cryptic formula. *The Dybbuk,* translated and produced in America in 1925, and more recently produced as an opera, describes with singular power the possession of a living body by the evil soul of a dead man. Both golems and dybbuks are fixed types, and serve as frequent ingredients of later Jewish tradition.

7. Edgar Allan Poe

In the eighteen-thirties occurred a literary dawn directly affecting not only the history of the weird tale, but that of short fiction as a whole; and indirectly moulding the trends and fortunes of a great European aesthetic school. It is our good fortune as Americans to be able to claim that dawn as our own, for it came in the person of our illustrious and unfortunate fellow-countryman Edgar Allan Poe. Poe's fame has been subject to curious undulations, and it is now a fashion amongst the "advanced intelligentsia" to minimise his importance both as an artist and as an influence; but it would be hard for any mature and reflective critic to deny the tremendous value of his work and the pervasive potency of his mind as an opener of artistic vistas. True, his type of outlook may have been anticipated; but it was he who first realised its possibilities and gave it supreme form and systematic expression. True also, that subsequent writers may have produced greater single tales than his; but again we must comprehend that it was only he who taught them by example and precept the art which they, having the way cleared for them and given an explicit guide, were perhaps able to carry to greater lengths. Whatever his limitations, Poe did that which no one else ever did or could have done; and to him we owe the modern horror-story in its final and perfected state.

Before Poe the bulk of weird writers had worked largely in the dark; without an understanding of the psychological basis of the horror appeal, and hampered by more or less of conformity to certain empty literary conventions such as the happy ending, virtue rewarded, and in general a hollow moral didacticism, acceptance of popular standards and values, and striving of the author to obtrude his own emotions into the story and take sides with the partisans of the majority's artificial ideas. Poe, on the other hand, perceived the essential impersonality of the real artist; and knew that the function of creative fiction is merely to express and interpret events and sensations as they are, regardless of how they tend or what they prove—good or evil, attractive or repulsive, stimulating or depressing—with the author always acting as a vivid and detached chronicler rather than as a teacher, sympathiser, or vendor of opinion. He saw clearly that all phases of life and thought are equally eligible as subject-matter for the artist, and being inclined by temperament to strangeness and gloom, decided to be the interpreter of those powerful feeling, and frequent happenings which attend pain rather than pleasure, decay rather than growth, terror rather than tranquillity, and which are fundamentally either adverse or indifferent to the tastes and traditional outward sentiments of mankind, and to the health, sanity, and normal expansive welfare of the species.

Poe's spectres thus acquired a convincing malignity possessed by none of their predecessors, and established a new standard of realism in the annals of literary horror. The impersonal and artistic intent, moreover, was aided by a scientific attitude not often found before; whereby Poe studied the human mind rather than the usages of Gothic fiction, and worked with an analytical knowledge of terror's true sources which doubled the force of his narratives and emancipated him from all the absurdities inherent in merely conventional shudder-coining. This example having been set, later authors were naturally forced to conform to it in order to compete at all; so that in this way a definite change began to affect the main stream of macabre writing. Poe, too, set a fashion in consummate craftsmanship; and although today some of his own work seems slightly melodramatic and unsophisticated, we can constantly trace his influence in such things as the maintenance of a single mood and achievement of a single impression in a tale, and the rigorous paring down of incidents to such as have a direct bearing on the plot and will figure prominently in the climax. Truly may it be said that Poe invented the short story in its present form. His elevation of disease, perversity, and decay to the level of artistically expressible themes was likewise infinitely far-reaching in effect; for avidly seized, sponsored, and intensified by his eminent French admirer Charles Pierre Baudelaire, it became the nucleus of the principal aesthetic movements in France, thus making Poe in a sense the father of the Decadents and the Symbolists.

Poet and critic by nature and supreme attainment, logician and philosopher by taste and mannerism, Poe was by no means immune from defects and affectations. His pretence to profound and obscure scholarship, his blundering ventures in stilted and laboured pseudo-humour, and his often vitriolic outbursts of critical prejudice must all be recognised and forgiven. Beyond and above them, and dwarfing them to insignificance, was a master's vision of the terror that stalks about and within us, and the worm that writhes and slavers in the hideously close abyss. Penetrating to every festering horror in the gaily painted mockery called existence, and in the solemn masquerade called human thought and feelings that vision had power to project itself in blackly magical crystallisations and transmutations; till there bloomed in the sterile America of the 'thirties and 'forties such a moonnourished garden of gorgeous poison fungi as not even the nether slope of Saturn might boast. Verses and tales alike sustain the burthen of cosmic panic. The raven whose noisome beak pierces the heart, the ghouls that toll iron bells in pestilential steeples, the vault of Ulalume in the black October night, the shocking spires and domes under the sea, the "wild, weird clime that lieth, sublime, out of Space—out of Time"—all these things and more leer at us amidst maniacal rattlings in the seething nightmare of the poetry. And in the prose there yawn open for us the very jaws of the pit—inconceivable abnormalities slyly hinted into a horrible half-knowledge by words whose innocence we scarcely doubt till the cracked tension of the speaker's hollow voice bids us fear their nameless implications; daemoniac patterns and presences slumbering noxiously till waked for one phobic instant into a shrieking revelation that cackles itself to sudden madness or explodes in memorable and cataclysmic echoes. A Witches' Sabbath of horror flinging off decorous robes is flashed before us—a sight the more monstrous because of the scientific skill with which every particular is marshalled and brought into an easy apparent relation to the known gruesomeness of material life.

Poe's tales, of course, fall into several classes; some of which contain a purer essence of spiritual horror than others. The tales of logic and ratiocination, forerunners of the modern detective story, are not to be included at all in weird literature; whilst certain others, probably influenced considerably by Hoffmann, possess an extravagance which relegates them to the borderline of the grotesque. Still a third group deal with abnormal psychology and monomania in such a way as to express terror but not weirdness. A substantial residuum, however, represent the literature of supernatural horror in its acutest form; and give their author a permanent and unassailable place as deity and fountain-head of all modern diabolic fiction. Who can forget the terrible swollen ship poised on the billow-chasm's edge in "MS. Found in a Bottle"—the dark intimations of her unhallowed age and monstrous growth, her sinister crew of unseeing greybeards, and her frightful southward rush under full sail through the ice of the Antarctic night, sucked onward by some resistless devil-current toward a vortex of eldritch enlightenment which must end in destruction? Then there is the unutterable "M. Valdemar", kept together by hypnotism for seven months after his death, and uttering frantic sounds but a moment before the breaking of the spell leaves him "a nearly liquid mass of loathsome—of detestable putrescence". In the *Narrative of A. Gordon Pym* the voyagers reach first a strange south polar land of murderous savages where nothing is white and where vast rocky ravines have the form of titanic Egyptian letters spelling terrible primal arcana of earth; and thereafter a still more mysterious realm where everything is white, and where shrouded giants and snowy-plumed birds guard a cryptic cataract of mist which empties from immeasurable celestial heights into a torrid milky sea. "Metzengerstein" horrifies with its malign hints of a monstrous metempsychosis—the mad nobleman who burns the stable of his hereditary foe; the colossal unknown horse that issues from the blazing building after the owner has perished therein; the vanishing bit of ancient tapestry where was shewn the giant horse of the victim's ancestor in the Crusades; the madman's wild and constant riding on the great horse, and his fear and hatred of the steed; the meaningless prophecies that brood obscurely over the warring houses; and finally, the burning of the madman's palace and the death therein of the owner, borne helpless into the flames and up the vast staircases astride the beast he has ridden so strangely. Afterward the rising smoke of the ruins takes the form of a gigantic horse. "The Man of the Crowd", telling of one who roams day and night to mingle with streams of people as if afraid to be alone, has quieter effects, but implies nothing less of cosmic fear. Poe's mind was never far from terror and decay, and we see in every tale, poem, and philosophical dialogue a tense eagerness to fathom unplumbed wells of night, to pierce the veil of death, and to reign in fancy as lord of the frightful mysteries of time and space.

Certain of Poe's tales possess an almost absolute perfection of artistic form which makes them veritable beacon-lights in the province of the short story. Poe could, when he wished, give to his prose a richly poetic cast; employing that archaic and Orientalised style with jewelled phrase, quasi-Biblical repetition, and recurrent burthen so successfully used by later writers like Oscar Wilde and Lord Dunsany; and in the cases where he has done this we have an effect of lyrical phantasy almost narcotic in essence—an opium pageant of dream in the language of dream, with every unnatural colour and grotesque image bodied forth in a symphony of corresponding sound. "The Masque of the Red Death", "Silence—A Fable", and "Shadow—A Parable" are assuredly poems in every sense of the word save the metrical one, and owe as much of their power to aural cadence as to visual imagery. But it is in two of the less openly poetic tales, "Ligeia" and "The Fall of the House of Usher"—especially the latter—that one finds those very summits of artistry whereby Poe takes his place at the head of fictional miniaturists. Simple and straightforward in plot, both of these tales owe their supreme magic to the cunning development which appears in the selection and collocation of every least incident. "Ligeia" tells of a first wife of lofty and mysterious origin, who after death returns through a preternatural force of will to take possession of the body of a second wife; imposing even her physical appearance on the temporary reanimated corpse of her victim at the last moment. Despite a suspicion of prolixity and topheaviness, the narrative reaches its terrific climax with relentless power. "Usher", whose superiority in detail and proportion is very marked, hints shudderingly of obscure life in inorganic things, and displays an abnormally linked trinity of entities at the end of a long and isolated family history—a brother, his twin sister, and their incredibly ancient house all sharing a single soul and meeting one common dissolution at the same moment.

These bizarre conceptions, so awkward in unskilful hands, become under Poe's spell living and convincing terrors to haunt our nights; and all because the author understood so perfectly the very mechanics and physiology of fear and strangeness— the essential details to emphasise, the precise incongruities and conceits to select as preliminaries or concomitants to horror, the exact incidents and allusions to throw out innocently in advance as symbols or prefigurings of each major step toward the hideous denouement to come, the nice adjustments of cumulative force and the unerring accuracy in linkage of parts which make for faultless unity throughout and thunderous effectiveness at the climactic moment, the delicate nuances of scenic and landscape value to select in establishing and sustaining the desired mood and vitalising the desired illusion—principles of this kind, and dozens of obscurer ones too elusive to be described or even fully comprehended by any ordinary commentator. Melodrama and unsophistication there may be—we are told of one fastidious Frenchman who could not bear to read Poe except in Baudelaire's urbane and Gallically modulated translation—but all traces of such things are wholly overshadowed by a potent and inborn sense of the spectral, the morbid, and the horrible which gushed forth from every cell of the artist's creative mentality and stamped his macabre work with the ineffaceable mark of supreme genius. Poe's weird tales are *alive* in a manner that few others can ever hope to be.

Like most fantaisistes, Poe excels in incidents and broad narrative effects rather than in character drawing. His typical protagonist is generally a dark, handsome, proud, melancholy, intellectual, highly sensitive, capricious, introspective, isolated, and sometimes slightly mad gentleman of ancient family and opulent circumstances; usually deeply learned in strange lore, and darkly ambitious of penetrating to forbidden secrets of the universe. Aside from a high-sounding name, this character obviously derives little from the early Gothic novel; for he is clearly neither the wooden hero nor the diabolical villain of Radcliffian or Ludovician romance. Indirectly, however, he does possess a sort of genealogical connexion; since his gloomy, ambitious, and anti-social qualities savour strongly of the typical Byronic hero, who in turn is definitely an offspring of the Gothic Manfreds, Montonis, and Ambrosios. More particular qualities appear to be derived from the psychology of Poe himself, who certainly possessed much of the depression, sensitiveness, mad aspiration, loneliness, and extravagant freakishness which he attributes to his haughty and solitary victims of Fate.

8. The Weird Tradition in America

The public for whom Poe wrote, though grossly unappreciative of his art, was by no means unaccustomed to the horrors with which he dealt. America, besides inheriting the usual dark folklore of Europe, had an additional fund of weird associations to draw upon; so that spectral legends had already been recognised as fruitful subject-matter for literature. Charles Brockden Brown had achieved phenomenal fame with his Radcliffian romances, and Washington Irving's lighter treatment of eerie themes had quickly become classic. This additional fund proceeded, as Paul Elmer More has pointed out, from the keen spiritual and theological interests of the first colonists, plus the strange and forbidding nature of the scene into which they were plunged. The vast and gloomy virgin forests in whose perpetual twilight all terrors might well lurk; the hordes of coppery Indians whose strange, saturnine visages and violent customs hinted strongly at traces of infernal origin; the free rein given under the influence of Puritan theocracy to all manner of notions respecting man's relation to the stern and vengeful God of the Calvinists, and to the sulphureous Adversary of that God, about whom so much was thundered in the pulpits each Sunday; and the morbid introspection developed by an isolated backwoods life devoid of normal amusements and of the recreational mood, harassed by commands for theological self-examination, keyed to unnatural emotional repression, and forming above all a mere grim struggle for survival—all these things conspired to produce an environment in which the black whisperings of sinister grandams were heard far beyond the chimney corner, and in which tales of witchcraft and unbelievable secret monstrosities lingered long after the dread days of the Salem nightmare.

Poe represents the newer, more disillusioned, and more technically finished of the weird schools that rose out of this propitious milieu. Another school—the tradition of moral values, gentle restraint, and mild, leisurely phantasy tinged more or less with the whimsical—was represented by another famous, misunderstood, and lonely figure in American letters—the shy and sensitive Nathaniel Hawthorne, scion of antique Salem and great-grandson of one of the bloodiest of the old witchcraft judges. In Hawthorne we have none of the violence, the daring, the high colouring, the intense dramatic sense, the cosmic malignity, and the undivided and impersonal artistry of Poe. Here, instead, is a gentle soul cramped by the Puritanism of early New England; shadowed and wistful, and grieved at an unmoral universe which everywhere transcends the conventional patterns thought by our forefathers to represent divine and immutable law. Evil, a very real force to Hawthorne, appears on every hand as a lurking and conquering adversary; and the visible world becomes in his fancy a theatre of infinite tragedy and woe, with unseen half-existent influences hovering over it and through it, battling for supremacy and moulding the destinies of the hapless mortals who form its vain and self-deluded population. The heritage of American weirdness was his to a most intense degree, and he saw a dismal throng of vague spectres behind the common phenomena of life; but he was not disinterested enough to value impressions, sensations, and beauties of narration for their own sake. He must needs weave his phantasy into some quietly melancholy fabric of didactic or allegorical cast, in which his meekly resigned cynicism may display with naive moral appraisal the perfidy of a human race which he cannot cease to cherish and mourn despite his insight into its hypocrisy. Supernatural horror, then, is never a primary object with Hawthorne; though its impulses were so deeply woven into his personality that he cannot help suggesting it with the force of genius when he calls upon the unreal world to illustrate the pensive sermon he wishes to preach.

Hawthorne's intimations of the weird, always gentle, elusive, and restrained, may be traced throughout his work. The mood that produced them found one delightful vent in the Teutonised retelling of classic myths for children contained in *A Wonder Book* and *Tanglewood Tales*, and at other times exercised itself in casting a certain strangeness and intangible witchery or malevolence over events not meant to be actually supernatural; as in the macabre posthumous novel *Dr. Grimshawe's Secret*, which invests with a peculiar sort of repulsion a house existing to this day in Salem, and abutting on the ancient Charter Street Burying Ground. In *The Marble Faun*, whose design was sketched out in an Italian villa reputed to be haunted, a tremendous background of genuine phantasy and mystery palpitates just beyond the common reader's sight; and glimpses of fabulous blood in mortal veins are hinted at during the course of a romance which cannot help being interesting despite the persistent incubus of moral allegory, anti-Popery propaganda, and a Puritan prudery which has caused the late D. H. Lawrence to express a longing to treat the author in a highly undignified manner. *Septimius Felton*, a posthumous novel whose idea was to have been elaborated and incorporated into the unfinished *Dolliver Romance*, touches on the Elixir of Life in a more or less capable fashion; whilst the notes for a never-written tale to be called "The Ancestral Footstep" shew what Hawthorne would have done with an intensive treatment of an old English superstition—that of an ancient and accursed line whose members left footprints of blood as they walked—which appears incidentally in both *Septimius Felton* and *Dr. Grimshawe's Secret*.

Many of Hawthorne's shorter tales exhibit weirdness, either of atmosphere or of incident, to a remarkable degree. "Edward Randolph's Portrait", in *Legends of the Province House*, has its diabolic moments. "The Minister's Black Veil" (founded on an actual incident) and "The Ambitious Guest" imply much more than they state, whilst "Ethan Brand"—a fragment of a longer work never completed—rises to genuine heights of cosmic fear with its vignette of the wild hill country and the blazing, desolate lime-kilns, and its delineation of the Byronic "unpardonable sinner", whose troubled life ends with a peal of fearful laughter in the night as he seeks rest amidst the flames of the furnace. Some of Hawthorne's notes tell of weird tales he would have written had he lived longer—an especially vivid plot being that concerning a baffling stranger who appeared now and then in public assemblies, and who was at last followed and found to come and go from a very ancient grave.

But foremost as a finished, artistic unit among all our author's weird material is the famous and exquisitely wrought novel, *The House of the Seven Gables*, in which the relentless working out of an ancestral curse is developed with astonishing power against the sinister background of a very ancient Salem house—one of those peaked Gothic affairs which formed the first regular building-up of our New England coast towns, but which gave way after the seventeenth century to the more familiar gambrel-roofed or classic Georgian types now known as "Colonial". Of these old gabled Gothic houses scarcely a dozen are to be seen today in their original condition throughout the United States, but one well known to Hawthorne still stands in Turner

Street, Salem, and is pointed out with doubtful authority as the scene and inspiration of the romance. Such an edifice, with its spectral peaks, its clustered chimneys, its overhanging second story, its grotesque corner-brackets, and its diamond-paned lattice windows, is indeed an object well calculated to evoke sombre reflections; typifying as it does the dark Puritan age of concealed horror and witch-whispers which preceded the beauty, rationality, and spaciousness of the eighteenth century. Hawthorne saw many in his youth, and knew the black tales connected with some of them. He heard, too, many rumours of a curse upon his own line as the result of his great-grandfather's severity as a witchcraft judge in 1692.

From this setting came the immortal tale—New England's greatest contribution to weird literature—and we can feel in an instant the authenticity of the atmosphere presented to us. Stealthy horror and disease lurk within the weather-blackened, moss-crusted, and elm-shadowed walls of the archaic dwelling so vividly displayed, and we grasp the brooding malignity of the place when we read that its builder—old Colonel Pyncheon—snatched the land with peculiar ruthlessness from its original settler, Matthew Maule, whom he condemned to the gallows as a wizard in the year of the panic. Maule died cursing old Pyncheon—"God will give him blood to drink"— and the waters of the old well on the seized land turned bitter. Maule's carpenter son consented to build the great gabled house for his father's triumphant enemy, but the old Colonel died strangely on the day of its dedication. Then followed generations of odd vicissitudes, with queer whispers about the dark powers of the Maules, and peculiar and sometimes terrible ends befalling the Pyncheons.

The overshadowing malevolence of the ancient house—almost as alive as Poe's House of Usher, though in a subtler way—pervades the tale as a recurrent motif pervades an operatic tragedy; and when the main story is reached, we behold the modern Pyncheons in a pitiable state of decay. Poor old Hepzibah, the eccentric reduced gentlewoman; child-like, unfortunate Clifford, just released from undeserved imprisonment; sly and treacherous Judge Pyncheon, who is the old Colonel all over again—all these figures are tremendous symbols, and are well matched by the stunted vegetation and anaemic fowls in the garden. It was almost a pity to supply a fairly happy ending, with a union of sprightly Phoebe, cousin and last scion of the Pyncheons, to the prepossessing young man who turns out to be the last of the Maules. This union, presumably, ends the curse. Hawthorne avoids all violence of diction or movement, and keeps his implications of terror well in the background; but occasional glimpses amply serve to sustain the mood and redeem the work from pure allegorical aridity. Incidents like the bewitching of Alice Pyncheon in the early eighteenth century, and the spectral music of her harpsichord which precedes a death in the family—the latter a variant of an immemorial type of Aryan myth—link the action directly with the supernatural; whilst the dead nocturnal vigil of old Judge Pyncheon in the ancient parlour, with his frightfully ticking watch, is stark horror of the most poignant and genuine sort. The way in which the Judge's death is first adumbrated by the motions and sniffing of a strange cat outside the window, long before the fact is suspected either by the reader or by any of the characters, is a stroke of genius which Poe could not have surpassed. Later the strange cat watches intently outside that same window in the night and on the next day, for—something. It is clearly the psychopomp of primeval myth, fitted and adapted with infinite deftness to its latter-day setting.

But Hawthorne left no well-defined literary posterity. His mood and attitude belonged to the age which closed with him, and it is the spirit of Poe—who so clearly and realistically understood the natural basis of the horror-appeal and the correct mechanics of its achievement—which survived and blossomed. Among the earliest of Poe's disciples may be reckoned the brilliant young Irishman Fitz-James O'Brien (1828–1862), who became naturalised as an American and perished honourably in the Civil War. It is he who gave us "What Was It?", the first well-shaped short story of a tangible but invisible being, and the prototype of de Maupassant's "Horla"; he also who created the inimitable "Diamond Lens", in which a young microscopist falls in love with a maiden of an infinitesimal world which he has discovered in a drop of water. O'Brien's early death undoubtedly deprived us of some masterful tales of strangeness and terror, though his genius was not, properly speaking, of the same titan quality which characterised Poe and Hawthorne.

Closer to real greatness was the eccentric and saturnine journalist Ambrose Bierce, born in 1842; who likewise entered the Civil War, but survived to write some immortal tales and to disappear in 1913 in as great a cloud of mystery as any he ever evoked from his nightmare fancy. Bierce was a satirist and pamphleteer of note, but the bulk of his artistic reputation must rest upon his grim and savage short stories; a large number of which deal with the Civil War and form the most vivid and realistic expression which that conflict has yet received in fiction. Virtually all of Bierce's tales are tales of horror; and whilst many of them treat only of the physical and psychological horrors within Nature, a substantial proportion admit the malignly supernatural and form a leading element in America's fund of weird literature. Mr. Samuel Loveman, a living poet and critic who was personally acquainted with Bierce, thus sums up the genius of the great shadow-maker in the preface to some of his letters:

"In Bierce, the evocation of horror becomes for the first time, not so much the prescription or perversion of Poe and Maupassant, but an atmosphere definite and uncannily precise. Words, so simple that one would be prone to ascribe them to the limitations of a literary hack, take on an unholy horror, a new and unguessed transformation. In Poe one finds it a *tour de force,* in Maupassant a nervous engagement of the flagellated climax. To Bierce, simply and sincerely, diabolism held in its tormented depth, a legitimate and reliant means to the end yet a tacit confirmation with Nature is in every instance insisted upon.

"In 'The Death of Halpin Frayser', flowers, verdure, and the boughs and leaves of trees are magnificently placed as an opposing foil to unnatural malignity. Not the accustomed golden world, but a world pervaded with the mystery of blue and the breathless recalcitrance of dreams, is Bierce's. Yet, curiously, inhumanity is not altogether absent."

The "inhumanity" mentioned by Mr. Loveman finds vent in a rare strain of sardonic comedy and graveyard humour, and a kind of delight in images of cruelty and tantalising disappointment. The former quality is well illustrated by some of the subtitles in the darker narratives; such as "One does not always eat what is on the table", describing a body laid out for a coroner's inquest, and "A man though naked may be in rags", referring to a frightfully mangled corpse.

Bierce's work is in general somewhat uneven. Many of the stories are obviously mechanical, and marred by a jaunty and commonplacely artificial style derived from journalistic models; but the grim malevolence stalking through all of them is unmistakable, and several stand out as permanent mountain-peaks of American weird writing. "The Death of Halpin Frayser", called by Frederic Taber Cooper the most fiendishly ghastly tale in the literature of the Anglo-Saxon race, tells of a body skulking by night without a soul in a weird and horribly ensanguined wood, and of a man beset by ancestral memories who met death at the claws of that which had been his fervently loved mother. "The Damned Thing", frequently copied in popular anthologies, chronicles the hideous devastations of an invisible entity that waddles and flounders on the hills and in the wheatfields by night and day. "The Suitable Surroundings" evokes with singular subtlety yet apparent simplicity a piercing sense of the terror which may reside in the written word. In the story the weird author Colston says to his friend Marsh, "You are brave enough to read me in a street-car, but—in a deserted house—alone—in the forest—at night! Bah! I have a manuscript in my pocket that would kill you!" Marsh reads the manuscript in "the suitable surroundings"—and it does kill him. "The Middle Toe of the Right Foot" is clumsily developed, but has a powerful climax. A man named Manton has horribly killed his two children and his wife, the latter of whom lacked the middle toe of the right foot. Ten years later he returns much altered to the neighbourhood; and, being secretly recognised, is provoked into a bowie-knife duel in the dark, to be held in the now abandoned house where his crime was committed. When the moment of the duel arrives a trick is played upon him; and he is left without an antagonist, shut in a night-black ground floor room of the reputedly haunted edifice, with the thick dust of a decade on every hand. No knife is drawn against him, for only a thorough scare is intended; but on the next day he is found crouched in a corner with distorted face, dead of sheer fright at something he has seen. The only clue visible to the discoverers is one having terrible implications: "In the dust of years that lay thick upon the floor—leading from the door by which they had entered, straight across the room to within a yard of Manton's crouching corpse—were three parallel lines of footprints—light but definite impressions of bare feet, the outer ones those of small children, the inner a woman's. From the point at which they ended they did not return; they pointed all one way." And, of course, the woman's prints shewed a lack of the middle toe of the right foot. "The Spook House", told with a severely homely air of journalistic verisimilitude, conveys terrible hints of shocking mystery. In 1858 an entire family of seven persons disappears suddenly and unaccountably from a plantation house in eastern Kentucky, leaving all its possessions untouched—furniture, clothing, food supplies, horses, cattle, and slaves. About a year later two men of high standing are forced by a storm to take shelter in the deserted dwelling, and in so doing stumble into a strange subterranean room lit by an unaccountable greenish light and having an iron door which cannot be opened from within. In this room lie the decayed corpses of all the missing family; and as one of the discoverers rushes forward to embrace a body he seems to recognise, the other is so overpowered by a strange foetor that he accidentally shuts his companion in the vault and loses consciousness. Recovering his senses six weeks later, the survivor is unable to find the hidden room; and the house is burned during the Civil War. The imprisoned discoverer is never seen or heard of again.

Bierce seldom realises the atmospheric possibilities of his themes as vividly as Poe; and much of his work contains a certain touch of naiveté, prosaic angularity, or early-American provincialism which contrasts somewhat with the efforts of later horror-masters. Nevertheless the genuineness and artistry of his dark intimations are always unmistakable, so that his greatness is in no danger of eclipse. As arranged in his definitively collected works, Bierce's weird tales occur mainly in two volumes, *Can Such Things Be?* and *In the Midst of Life*. The former, indeed, is almost wholly given over to the supernatural.

Much of the best in American horror-literature has come from pens not mainly devoted to that medium. Oliver Wendell Holmes's historic *Elsie Venner* suggests with admirable restraint an unnatural ophidian element in a young woman pre-natally influenced, and sustains the atmosphere with finely discriminating landscape touches. In *The Turn of the Screw* Henry James triumphs over his inevitable pomposity and prolixity sufficiently well to create a truly potent air of sinister menace; depicting the hideous influence of two dead and evil servants, Peter Quint and the governess Miss Jessel, over a small boy and girl who had been under their care. James is perhaps too diffuse, too unctuously urbane, and too much addicted to subtleties of speech to realise fully all the wild and devastating horror in his situations; but for all that there is a rare and mounting tide of fright, culminating in the death of the little boy, which gives the novelette a permanent place in its special class.

F. Marion Crawford produced several weird tales of varying quality, now collected in a volume entitled *Wandering Ghosts*. "For the Blood Is the Life" touches powerfully on a case of moon-cursed vampirism near an ancient tower on the rocks of the lonely South Italian sea-coast. "The Dead Smile" treats of family horrors in an old house and an ancestral vault in Ireland, and introduces the banshee with considerable force. "The Upper Berth", however, is Crawford's weird masterpiece; and is one of the most tremendous horror-stories in all literature. In this tale of a suicide-haunted stateroom such things as the spectral salt-water dampness, the strangely open porthole, and the nightmare struggle with the nameless object are handled with incomparable dexterity.

Very genuine, though not without the typical mannered extravagance of the eighteen-nineties, is the strain of horror in the early work of Robert W. Chambers, since renowned for products of a very different quality. *The King in Yellow*, a series of vaguely connected short stories having as a background a monstrous and suppressed book whose perusal brings fright, madness, and spectral tragedy, really achieves notable heights of cosmic fear in spite of uneven interest and a somewhat trivial and affected cultivation of the Gallic studio atmosphere made popular by Du Maurier's *Trilby*. The most powerful of its tales, perhaps, is "The Yellow Sign", in which is introduced a silent and terrible churchyard watchman with a face like a puffy grave-worm's. A boy, describing a tussle he has had with this creature, shivers and sickens as he relates a certain detail. "Well, sir, it's Gawd's truth that when I 'it 'im 'e grabbed me wrists, sir, and when I twisted 'is soft, mushy fist one of 'is fingers come off in me 'and." An artist, who after seeing him has shared with another a strange dream of a nocturnal hearse, is shocked by the voice with which the watchman accosts him. The fellow emits a muttering sound that fills the head like thick oily smoke from a fat-rendering vat or an odour of noisome decay. What he mumbles is merely this: "Have you found the Yellow Sign?"

A weirdly hieroglyphed onyx talisman, picked up in the street by the sharer of his dream, is shortly given the artist; and after stumbling queerly upon the hellish and forbidden book of horrors the two learn, among other hideous things which no sane mortal should know, that this talisman is indeed the nameless Yellow Sign handed down from the accursed cult of Hastur—from primordial Carcosa, whereof the volume treats, and some nightmare memory of which seems to lurk latent and ominous at the back of all men's minds. Soon they hear the rumbling of the black-plumed hearse driven by the flabby and corpse-faced watchman. He enters the night-shrouded house in quest of the Yellow Sign, all bolts and bars rotting at his touch. And when the people rush in, drawn by a scream that no human throat could utter, they find three forms on the floor—two dead and one dying. One of the dead shapes is far gone in decay. It is the churchyard watchman, and the doctor exclaims, "That man must have been dead for months." It is worth observing that the author derives most of the names and allusions connected with his eldritch land of primal memory from the tales of Ambrose Bierce. Other early works of Mr. Chambers displaying the outré and macabre element are *The Maker of Moons* and *In Search of the Unknown*. One cannot help regretting that he did not further develop a vein in which he could so easily have become a recognised master.

Horror material of authentic force may be found in the work of the New England realist Mary E. Wilkins; whose volume of short tales, *The Wind in the Rose-Bush*, contains a number of noteworthy achievements. In "The Shadows on the Wall" we are shewn with consummate skill the response of a staid New England household to uncanny tragedy; and the sourceless shadow of the poisoned brother well prepares us for the climactic moment when the shadow of the secret murderer, who has killed himself in a neighbouring city, suddenly appears beside it. Charlotte Perkins Gilman, in "The Yellow Wall Paper", rises to a classic level in subtly delineating the madness which crawls over a woman dwelling in the hideously papered room where a madwoman was once confined.

In "The Dead Valley" the eminent architect and mediaevalist Ralph Adams Cram achieves a memorably potent degree of vague regional horror through subtleties of atmosphere and description.

Still further carrying on our spectral tradition is the gifted and versatile humourist Irvin S. Cobb, whose work both early and recent contains some finely weird specimens. "Fishhead", an early achievement, is banefully effective in its portrayal of unnatural affinities between a hybrid idiot and the strange fish of an isolated lake, which at the last avenge their biped kinsman's murder. Later work of Mr. Cobb introduces an element of possible science, as in the tale of hereditary memory where a modern man with a negroid strain utters words in African jungle speech when run down by a train under visual and aural circumstances recalling the maiming of his black ancestor by a rhinoceros a century before.

Extremely high in artistic stature is the novel *The Dark Chamber* (1927), by the late Leonard Cline. This is the tale of a man who—with the characteristic ambition of the Gothic or Byronic hero-villain—seeks to defy Nature and recapture every moment of his past life through the abnormal stimulation of memory. To this end he employs endless notes, records, mnemonic objects, and pictures—and finally odours, music, and exotic drugs. At last his ambition goes beyond his personal life and reaches toward the black abysses of *hereditary* memory—even back to pre-human days amidst the steaming swamps of the Carboniferous age, and to still more unimaginable deeps of primal time and entity. He calls for madder music and takes stronger drugs, and finally his great dog grows oddly afraid of him. A noxious animal stench encompasses him, and he grows vacant-faced and sub-human. In the end he takes to the woods, howling at night beneath windows. He is finally found in a thicket, mangled to death. Beside him is the mangled corpse of his dog. They have killed each other. The atmosphere of this novel is malevolently potent, much attention being paid to the central figure's sinister home and household.

A less subtle and well-balanced but nevertheless highly effective creation is Herbert S. Gorman's novel, *The Place Called Dagon,* which relates the dark history of a western Massachusetts backwater where the descendants of refugees from the Salem witchcraft still keep alive the morbid and degenerate horrors of the Black Sabbat.

Sinister House, by Leland Hall, has touches of magnificent atmosphere but is marred by a somewhat mediocre romanticism.

Very notable in their way are some of the weird conceptions of the novelist and short-story writer Edward Lucas White, most of whose themes arise from actual dreams. "The Song of the Sirens" has a very pervasive strangeness, while such things as "Lukundoo" and "The Snout" rouse darker apprehensions. Mr. White imparts a very peculiar quality to his tales—an oblique sort of glamour which has its own distinctive type of convincingness.

Of younger Americans, none strikes the note of cosmic terror so well as the California poet, artist, and fictionist Clark Ashton Smith, whose bizarre writings, drawings, paintings, and stories are the delight of a sensitive few. Mr. Smith has for his background a universe of remote and paralysing fright—jungles of poisonous and iridescent blossoms on the moons of Saturn, evil and grotesque temples in Atlantis, Lemuria, and forgotten elder worlds, and dank morasses of spotted death-fungi in spectral countries beyond earth's rim. His longest and most ambitious poem, *The Hashish-Eater,* is in pentameter blank verse; and opens up chaotic and incredible vistas of kaleidoscopic nightmare in the spaces between the stars. In sheer daemonic strangeness and fertility of conception, Mr. Smith is perhaps unexcelled by any other writer dead or living. Who else has seen such gorgeous, luxuriant, and feverishly distorted visions of infinite spheres and multiple dimensions and lived to tell the tale? His short stories deal powerfully with other galaxies, worlds, and dimensions, as well as with strange regions and aeons on the earth. He tells of primal Hyperborea and its black amorphous god Tsathoggua; of the lost continent Zothique, and of the fabulous, vampire-curst land of Averoigne in mediaeval France. Some of Mr. Smith's best work can be found in the brochure entitled *The Double Shadow and Other Fantasies* (1933).

9. The Weird Tradition in the British Isles

Recent British literature, besides including the three or four greatest fantaisistes of the present age, has been gratifyingly fertile in the element of the weird. Rudyard Kipling has often approached it; and has, despite the omnipresent mannerisms, handled it with indubitable mastery in such tales as "The Phantom 'Rickshaw", "'The Finest Story in the World'", "The Recrudescence of Imray", and "The Mark of the Beast". This latter is of particular poignancy; the pictures of the naked leper-priest who mewed like an otter, of the spots which appeared on the chest of the man that priest cursed, of the growing carnivorousness of the victim and of the fear which horses began to display toward him, and of the eventually half-accomplished transformation of that victim into a leopard, being things which no reader is ever likely to forget. The final defeat of the malignant sorcery does not impair the force of the tale or the validity of its mystery.

Lafcadio Hearn, strange, wandering, and exotic, departs still farther from the realm of the real; and with the supreme artistry of a sensitive poet weaves phantasies impossible to an author of the solid roast-beef type. His *Fantastics,* written in America, contains some of the most impressive ghoulishness in all literature; whilst his *Kwaidan,* written in Japan, crystallises with matchless skill and delicacy the eerie lore and whispered legends of that richly colourful nation. Still more of Hearn's weird wizardry of language is shewn in some of his translations from the French, especially from Gautier and Flaubert. His version of the latter's *Temptation of St. Anthony* is a classic of fevered and riotous imagery clad in the magic of singing words.

Oscar Wilde may likewise be given a place amongst weird writers, both for certain of his exquisite fairy tales, and for his vivid *Picture of Dorian Gray,* in which a marvellous portrait for years assumes the duty of ageing and coarsening instead of its original, who meanwhile plunges into every excess of vice and crime without the outward loss of youth, beauty, and freshness. There is a sudden and potent climax when Dorian Gray, at last become a murderer, seeks to destroy the painting whose changes testify to his moral degeneracy. He stabs it with a knife, and a hideous cry and crash are heard; but when the servants enter they find it in all its pristine loveliness. "Lying on the floor was a dead man, in evening dress, with a knife in his heart. He was withered, wrinkled, and loathsome of visage. It was not till they had examined the rings that they recognised who it was."

Matthew Phipps Shiel, author of many weird, grotesque, and adventurous novels and tales, occasionally attains a high level of horrific magic. "Xélucha" is a noxiously hideous fragment, but is excelled by Mr. Shiel's undoubted masterpiece, "The House of Sounds", floridly written in the "yellow 'nineties", and re-cast with more artistic restraint in the early twentieth century. This story, in final form, deserves a place among the foremost things of its kind. It tells of a creeping horror and menace trickling down the centuries on a sub-arctic island off the coast of Norway; where, amidst the sweep of daemon winds and the ceaseless din of hellish waves and cataracts, a vengeful dead man built a brazen tower of terror. It is vaguely like, yet infinitely unlike, Poe's "Fall of the House of Usher". In the novel *The Purple Cloud* Mr. Shiel describes with tremendous power a curse which came out of the arctic to destroy mankind, and which for a time appears to have left but a single inhabitant on our planet. The sensations of this lone survivor as he realises his position, and roams through the corpse-littered and treasure-strown cities of the world as their absolute master, are delivered with a skill and artistry falling little short of actual majesty. Unfortunately the second half of the book, with its conventionally romantic element, involves a distinct "letdown".

Better known than Shiel is the ingenious Bram Stoker, who created many starkly horrific conceptions in a series of novels whose poor technique sadly impairs their net effect. *The Lair of the White Worm*, dealing with a gigantic primitive entity that lurks in a vault beneath an ancient castle, utterly ruins a magnificent idea by a development almost infantile. *The Jewel of Seven Stars*, touching on a strange Egyptian resurrection, is less crudely written. But best of all is the famous *Dracula*, which has become almost the standard modern exploitation of the frightful vampire myth. Count Dracula, a vampire, dwells in a horrible castle in the Carpathians; but finally migrates to England with the design of populating the country with fellow vampires. How an Englishman fares within Dracula's stronghold of terrors, and how the dead fiend's plot for domination is at last defeated, are elements which unite to form a tale now justly assigned a permanent place in English letters. *Dracula* evoked many similar novels of supernatural horror, among which the best are perhaps *The Beetle*, by Richard Marsh, *Brood of the Witch-Queen*, by "Sax Rohmer" (Arthur Sarsfield Ward), and *The Door of the Unreal*, by Gerald Biss. The latter handles quite dexterously the standard werewolf superstition. Much subtler and more artistic, and told with singular skill through the juxtaposed narratives of the several characters, is the novel *Cold Harbour*, by Francis Brett Young, in which an ancient house of strange malignancy is powerfully delineated. The mocking and well-nigh omnipotent fiend Humphrey Furnival holds echoes of the Manfred-Montoni type of early Gothic "villain", but is redeemed from triteness by many clever individualities. Only the slight diffuseness of explanation at the close, and the somewhat too free use of divination as a plot factor, keep this tale from approaching absolute perfection.

In the novel *Witch Wood* John Buchan depicts with tremendous force a survival of the evil Sabbat in a lonely district of Scotland. The description of the black forest with the evil stone, and of the terrible cosmic adumbrations when the horror is finally extirpated, will repay one for wading through the very gradual action and plethora of Scottish dialect. Some of Mr. Buchan's short stories are also extremely vivid in their spectral intimations; "The Green Wildebeest", a tale of African witchcraft, "The Wind in the Portico", with its awakening of dead Britanno-Roman horrors, and "Skule Skerry", with its touches of sub-arctic fright, being especially remarkable.

Clemence Housman, in the brief novelette "The Were-wolf", attains a high degree of gruesome tension and achieves to some extent the atmosphere of authentic folklore. In *The Elixir of Life* Arthur Ransome attains some darkly excellent effects despite a general naiveté of plot, while H. B. Drake's *The Shadowy Thing* summons up strange and terrible vistas. George Macdonald's *Lilith* has a compelling bizarrerie all its own; the first and simpler of the two versions being perhaps the more effective.

Deserving of distinguished notice as a forceful craftsman to whom an unseen mystic world is ever a close and vital reality is the poet Walter de la Mare, whose haunting verse and exquisite prose alike bear consistent traces of a strange vision reaching deeply into veiled spheres of beauty and terrible and forbidden dimensions of being. In the novel *The Return* we see the soul of a dead man reach out of its grave of two centuries and fasten itself upon the flesh of the living, so that even the face of the victim becomes that which had long ago returned to dust. Of the shorter tales, of which several volumes exist, many are unforgettable for their command of fear's and sorcery's darkest ramifications; notably "Seaton's Aunt", in which there lowers a noxious background of malignant vampirism; "The Tree", which tells of a frightful vegetable growth in the yard of a starving artist; "Out of the Deep", wherein we are given leave to imagine what thing answered the summons of a dying wastrel in a dark lonely house when he pulled a long-feared bell-cord in the attic chamber of his dread-haunted boyhood; "A Recluse", which hints at what sent a chance guest flying from a house in the night; "Mr. Kempe", which shews us a mad clerical hermit in quest of the human soul, dwelling in a frightful sea-cliff region beside an archaic abandoned chapel; and "All Hallows", a glimpse of daemoniac forces besieging a lonely mediaeval church and miraculously restoring the rotting masonry. De la Mare does not make fear the sole or even the dominant element of most of his tales, being apparently more interested in the subtleties of character involved. Occasionally he sinks to sheer whimsical phantasy of the Barrie order. Still, he is among the very few to whom unreality is a vivid, living presence; and as such he is able to put into his occasional fear-studies a keen potency which only a rare master can achieve. His poem "The Listeners" restores the Gothic shudder to modern verse.

The weird short story has fared well of late, an important contributor being the versatile E. F. Benson, whose "The Man Who Went Too Far" breathes whisperingly of a house at the edge of a dark wood, and of Pan's hoof-mark on the breast of a dead man. Mr. Benson's volume, *Visible and Invisible,* contains several stories of singular power; notably *"Negotium Perambulans",* whose unfolding reveals an abnormal monster from an ancient ecclesiastical panel which performs an act of miraculous vengeance in a lonely village on the Cornish coast, and "The Horror-Horn", through which lopes a terrible half-human survival dwelling on unvisited Alpine peaks. "The Face", in another collection, is lethally potent in its relentless aura of doom. H. R. Wakefield, in his collections *They Return at Evening* and *Others Who Return,* manages now and then to achieve great heights of horror despite a vitiating air of sophistication. The most notable stories are The Red Lodge with its slimy aqueous evil, "'He Cometh and He Passeth By'", "'And He Shall Sing . . .'", "The Cairn", "'Look Up There!'", "Blind Man's Buff", and that bit of lurking millennial horror, "The Seventeenth Hole at Duncaster". Mention has been made of the weird work of H. G. Wells and A. Conan Doyle. The former, in "The Ghost of Fear", reaches a very high level; while all the items in *Thirty Strange Stories* have strong fantastic implications. Doyle now and then struck a powerfully spectral note, as in "The Captain of the 'Pole-Star'", a tale of arctic ghostliness, and "Lot No. 249", wherein the reanimated mummy theme is used with more than ordinary skill. Hugh Walpole, of the same family as the founder of Gothic fiction, has sometimes approached the bizarre with much success; his short story "Mrs. Lunt" carrying a very poignant shudder. John Metcalfe, in the collection published as *The Smoking Leg,* attains now and then a rare pitch of potency; the tale entitled "The Bad Lands" containing graduations of horror that strongly savour of genius. More whimsical and inclined toward the amiable and innocuous phantasy of Sir J. M. Barrie are the short tales of E. M. Forster, grouped under the title of *The Celestial Omnibus*. Of these only one, dealing with a glimpse of Pan and his aura of fright, may be said to hold the true element of cosmic horror. Mrs. H. D. Everett, though adhering to very old and conventional models, occasionally reaches singular heights of spiritual terror in her collection of short stories. L. P. Hartley is notable for his incisive and extremely ghastly tale, "A Visitor from Down Under". May Sinclair's *Uncanny Stories* contain more of traditional occultism than of that creative treatment of fear which marks mastery in this field, and are inclined to lay more stress on human emotions and psychological delving than upon the stark phenomena of a cosmos utterly unreal. It may be well to remark here that occult believers are probably less effective than materialists in delineating the spectral and the fantastic, since to them the phantom world is so commonplace a reality that they tend to refer to it with less awe, remoteness, and impressiveness than do those who see in it an absolute and stupendous violation of the natural order.

Of rather uneven stylistic quality, but vast occasional power in its suggestion of lurking worlds and beings behind the ordinary surface of life, is the work of William Hope Hodgson, known today far less than it deserves to be. Despite a tendency toward conventionally sentimental conceptions of the universe, and of man's relation to it and to his fellows, Mr. Hodgson is perhaps second only to Algernon Blackwood in his serious treatment of unreality. Few can equal him in adumbrating the nearness of nameless forces and monstrous besieging entities through casual hints and insignificant details, or in conveying feelings of the spectral and the abnormal in connexion with regions or buildings.

In *The Boats of the "Glen Carrig"* (1907) we are shewn a variety of malign marvels and accursed unknown lands as encountered by the survivors of a sunken ship. The brooding menace in the earlier parts of the book is impossible to surpass, though a letdown in the direction of ordinary romance and adventure occurs toward the end. An inaccurate and pseudo-romantic attempt to reproduce eighteenth century prose detracts from the general effect, but the really profound nautical erudition everywhere displayed is a compensating factor.

The House on the Borderland (1908)—perhaps the greatest of all Mr. Hodgson's works—tells of a lonely and evilly regarded house in Ireland which forms a focus for hideous other-world forces and sustains a siege by blasphemous hybrid anomalies from a hidden abyss below. The wanderings of the narrator's spirit through limitless light-years of cosmic space and kalpas of eternity, and its witnessing of the solar system's final destruction, constitute something almost unique in standard literature. And everywhere there is manifest the author's power to suggest vague, ambushed horrors in natural scenery. But for a few touches of commonplace sentimentality this book would be a classic of the first water.

The Ghost Pirates (1909), regarded by Mr. Hodgson as rounding out a trilogy with the two previously mentioned works, is a powerful account of a doomed and haunted ship on its last voyage, and of the terrible sea-devils (of quasi-human aspect, and perhaps the spirits of bygone buccaneers) that besiege it and finally drag it down to an unknown fate. With its command of maritime knowledge, and its clever selection of hints and incidents suggestive of latent horrors in Nature, this book at times reaches enviable peaks of power.

The Night Land (1912) is a long-extended (583 pp.) tale of the earth's infinitely remote future—billions of billions of years ahead, after the death of the sun. It is told in a rather clumsy fashion, as the dreams of a man in the seventeenth century, whose mind merges with its own future incarnation; and is seriously marred by painful verboseness, repetitiousness, artificial and nauseously sticky romantic sentimentality, and an attempt at archaic language even more grotesque and absurd than that in *"Glen Carrig"*.

Allowing for all its faults, it is yet one of the most potent pieces of macabre imagination ever written. The picture of a night-black, dead planet, with the remains of the human race concentrated in a stupendously vast metal pyramid and besieged by monstrous, hybrid, and altogether unknown forces of the darkness, is something that no reader can ever forget. Shapes and entities of an altogether non-human and inconceivable sort—the prowlers of the black, man-forsaken, and unexplored world outside the pyramid—are *suggested* and *partly* described with ineffable potency; while the night-bound landscape with its chasms and slopes and dying volcanism takes on an almost sentient terror beneath the author's touch.

Midway in the book the central figure ventures outside the pyramid on a quest through death-haunted realms untrod by man for millions of years—and in his slow, minutely described, day-by-day progress over unthinkable leagues of immemorial blackness there is a sense of cosmic alienage, breathless mystery, and terrified expectancy unrivalled in the whole range of literature. The last quarter of the book drags woefully, but fails to spoil the tremendous power of the whole.

Mr. Hodgson's later volume, *Carnacki, the Ghost-Finder,* consists of several longish short stories published many years before in magazines. In quality it falls conspicuously below the level of the other books. We here find a more or less conventional stock figure of the "infallible detective" type—the progeny of M. Dupin and Sherlock Holmes—and the close kin of Algernon Blackwood's John Silence—moving through scenes and events badly marred by an atmosphere of professional "occultism". A few of the episodes, however, are of undeniable power; and afford glimpses of the peculiar genius characteristic of the author.

Naturally it is impossible in a brief sketch to trace out all the classic modern uses of the terror element. The ingredient must of necessity enter into all work both prose and verse treating broadly of life; and we are therefore not surprised to find a share in such writers as the poet Browning, whose "'Childe Roland to the Dark Tower Came'" is instinct with hideous menace, or the novelist Joseph Conrad, who often wrote of the dark secrets within the sea, and of the daemoniac driving power of Fate as influencing the lives of lonely and maniacally resolute men. Its trail is one of infinite ramifications; but we must here confine ourselves to its appearance in a relatively unmixed state, where it determines and dominates the work of art containing it.

Somewhat separate from the main British stream is that current of weirdness in Irish literature which came to the fore in the Celtic Renaissance of the later nineteenth and early twentieth centuries. Ghost and fairy lore have always been of great prominence in Ireland, and for over an hundred years have been recorded by a line of such faithful transcribers and translators as William Carleton, T. Crofton Croker, Lady Wilde—mother of Oscar Wilde—Douglas Hyde, and W. B. Yeats. Brought to notice by the modern movement, this body of myth has been carefully collected and studied;

and its salient features reproduced in the work of later figures like Yeats, J. M. Synge, "A. E.", Lady Gregory, Padraic Colum, James Stephens, and their colleagues.

Whilst on the whole more whimsically fantastic than terrible, such folklore and its consciously artistic counterparts contain much that falls truly within the domain of cosmic horror. Tales of burials in sunken churches beneath haunted lakes, accounts of death-heralding banshees and sinister changelings, ballads of spectres and "the unholy creatures of the raths"—all these have their poignant and definite shivers, and mark a strong and distinctive element in weird literature. Despite homely grotesqueness and absolute naivet,, there is genuine nightmare in the class of narrative represented by the yarn of Teig O'Kane, who in punishment for his wild life was ridden all night by a hideous corpse that demanded burial and drove him from churchyard to churchyard as the dead rose up loathsomely in each one and refused to accommodate the newcomer with a berth. Yeats, undoubtedly the greatest figure of the Irish revival if not the greatest of all living poets, has accomplished notable things both in original work and in the codification of old legends.

10. The Modern Masters

The best horror-tales of today, profiting by the long evolution of the type, possess a naturalness, convincingness, artistic smoothness, and skilful intensity of appeal quite beyond comparison with anything in the Gothic work of a century or more ago. Technique, craftsmanship, experience, and psychological knowledge have advanced tremendously with the passing years, so that much of the older work seems naive and artificial; redeemed, when redeemed at all, only by a genius which conquers heavy limitations. The tone of jaunty and inflated romance, full of false motivation and investing every conceivable event with a counterfeit significance and carelessly inclusive glamour, is now confined to lighter and more whimsical phases of supernatural writing. Serious weird stories are either made realistically intense by close consistency and perfect fidelity to Nature except in the one supernatural direction which the author allows himself, or else cast altogether in the realm of phantasy, with atmosphere cunningly adapted to the visualisation of a delicately exotic world of unreality beyond space and time, in which almost anything may happen if it but happen in true accord with certain types of imagination and illusion normal to the sensitive human brain. This, at least, is the dominant tendency; though of course many great contemporary writers slip occasionally into some of the flashy postures of immature romanticism, or into bits of the equally empty and absurd jargon of pseudo-scientific "occultism", now at one of its periodic high tides.

Of living creators of cosmic fear raised to its most artistic pitch, few if any can hope to equal the versatile Arthur Machen; author of some dozen tales long and short, in which the elements of hidden horror and brooding fright attain an almost incomparable substance and realistic acuteness. Mr. Machen, a general man of letters and master of an exquisitely lyrical and expressive prose style, has perhaps put more conscious effort into his picaresque *Chronicle of Clemendy*, his refreshing essays, his vivid autobiographical volumes, his fresh and spirited translations, and above all his memorable epic of the sensitive aesthetic mind, *The Hill of Dreams*, in which the youthful hero responds to the magic of that ancient Welsh environment which is the author's own, and lives a dream-life in the Roman city of Isca Silurum, now shrunk to the relic-strown village of Caerleon-on-Usk. But the fact remains that his powerful horror-material of the 'nineties and earlier nineteen-hundreds stands alone in its class, and marks a distinct epoch in the history of this literary form.

Mr. Machen, with an impressionable Celtic heritage linked to keen youthful memories of the wild domed hills, archaic forests, and cryptical Roman ruins of the Gwent countryside, has developed an imaginative life of rare beauty, intensity, and historic background. He has absorbed the mediaeval mystery of dark woods and ancient customs, and is a champion of the Middle Ages in all things—including the Catholic faith. He has yielded, likewise, to the spell of the Britanno-Roman life which once surged over his native region; and finds strange magic in the fortified camps, tessellated pavements, fragments of statues, and kindred things which tell of the day when classicism reigned and Latin was the language of the country. A young American poet, Frank Belknap Long, Jun., has well summarised this dreamer's rich endowments and wizardry of expression in the sonnet "On Reading Arthur Machen":

"There is a glory in the autumn wood;
The ancient lanes of England wind and climb
Past wizard oaks and gorse and tangled thyme
To where a fort of mighty empire stood:
There is a glamour in the autumn sky;
The reddened clouds are writhing in the glow
Of some great fire, and there are glints below
Of tawny yellow where the embers die.

I wait, for he will show me, clear and cold,
High-rais'd in splendour, sharp against the North,
The Roman eagles, and thro' mists of gold
The marching legions as they issue forth:
I wait, for I would share with him again
The ancient wisdom, and the ancient pain."

Of Mr. Machen's horror-tales the most famous is perhaps "The Great God Pan" (1894), which tells of a singular and terrible experiment and its consequences. A young woman, through surgery of the brain-cells, is made to see the vast and monstrous deity of Nature, and becomes an idiot in consequence, dying less than a year later. Years afterward a strange, ominous, and foreign-looking child named Helen Vaughan is placed to board with a family in rural Wales, and haunts the woods in unaccountable fashion. A little boy is thrown out of his mind at sight of someone or something he spies with her, and a young girl comes to a terrible end in similar fashion. All this mystery is strangely interwoven with the Roman rural deities of the place, as sculptured in antique fragments. After another lapse of years, a woman of strangely exotic beauty appears in society, drives her husband to horror and death, causes an artist to paint unthinkable paintings of Witches' Sabbaths, creates an epidemic of suicide among the men of her acquaintance, and is finally discovered to be a frequenter of the lowest dens of vice in London, where even the most callous degenerates are shocked at her enormities. Through the clever comparing of notes on the part of those who have had word of her at various stages of her career, this woman is discovered to be the girl Helen Vaughan; who is the child—by no mortal father—of the young woman on whom the brain experiment was made. She is a daughter of hideous Pan himself, and at the last is put to death amidst horrible transmutations of form involving changes of sex and a descent to the most primal manifestations of the life-principle.

But the charm of the tale is in the telling. No one could begin to describe the cumulative suspense and ultimate horror with which every paragraph abounds without following fully the precise order in which Mr. Machen unfolds his gradual hints and revelations. Melodrama is undeniably present, and coincidence is stretched to a length which appears absurd upon analysis; but in the malign witchery of the tale as a whole these trifles are forgotten, and the sensitive reader reaches the end with only an appreciative shudder and a tendency to repeat the words of one of the characters: "It is too incredible, too monstrous; such things can never be in this quiet world. . . . Why, man, if such a case were possible, our earth would be a nightmare."

Less famous and less complex in plot than "The Great God Pan", but definitely finer in atmosphere and general artistic value, is the curious and dimly disquieting chronicle called "The White People", whose central portion purports to be the diary or notes of a little girl whose nurse has introduced her to some of the forbidden magic and soul-blasting traditions of the noxious witch-cult—the cult whose whispered lore was handed down long lines of peasantry throughout Western Europe, and whose members sometimes stole forth at night, one by one, to meet in black woods and lonely places for the revolting orgies of the Witches' Sabbath. Mr. Machen's narrative, a triumph of skilful selectiveness and restraint, accumulates enormous power as it flows on in a stream of innocent childish prattle; introducing allusions to strange "nymphs", "Dôls", "voolas", "White, Green, and Scarlet Ceremonies", "Aklo letters", "Chian language", "Mao games", and the like. The rites learned by the nurse from her witch grandmother are taught to the child by the time she is three years old, and her artless accounts of the dangerous secret revelations possess a lurking terror generously mixed with pathos. Evil charms well known to anthropologists are described with juvenile naiveté, and finally there comes a winter afternoon journey into the old Welsh hills, performed under an imaginative spell which lends to the wild scenery an added weirdness, strangeness, and suggestion of grotesque sentience. The details of this journey are given with marvellous vividness, and form to the keen critic a masterpiece of fantastic writing, with almost unlimited power in the intimation of potent hideousness and cosmic aberration. At length the child—whose age is then thirteen—comes upon a cryptic and banefully beautiful thing in the midst of a dark and inaccessible wood. She flees in awe, but is permanently altered and repeatedly revisits the wood. In the end horror overtakes her in a manner deftly prefigured by an anecdote in the prologue, but she poisons herself in time. Like the mother of Helen Vaughan in The Great God Pan, she has seen that frightful deity. She is discovered dead in the dark wood beside the cryptic thing she found; and that thing—a whitely luminous statue of Roman workmanship about which dire mediaeval rumours had clustered—is affrightedly hammered into dust by the searchers.

In the episodic novel of *The Three Impostors,* a work whose merit as a whole is somewhat marred by an imitation of the jaunty Stevenson manner, occur certain tales which perhaps represent the high-water mark of Machen's skill as a terror-weaver. Here we find in its most artistic form a favourite weird conception of the author's; the notion that beneath the mounds and rocks of the wild Welsh hills dwell subterraneously that squat primitive race whose vestiges gave rise to our common folk legends of fairies, elves, and the "little people", and whose acts are even now responsible for certain unexplained disappearances, and occasional substitutions of strange dark "changelings" for normal infants. This theme receives its finest treatment in the episode entitled "The Novel of the Black Seal"; where a professor, having discovered a singular identity between certain characters scrawled on Welsh limestone rocks and those existing in a prehistoric black seal from Babylon, sets out on a course of discovery which leads him to unknown and terrible things. A queer passage in the ancient geographer Solinus, a series of mysterious disappearances in the lonely reaches of Wales, a strange idiot son born to a rural mother after a fright in which her inmost faculties were shaken; all these things suggest to the professor a hideous connexion and a condition revolting to any friend and respecter of the human race. He hires the idiot boy, who jabbers strangely at times in a repulsive hissing voice, and is subject to odd epileptic seizures. Once, after such a seizure in the professor's study by night, disquieting odours and evidences of unnatural presences are found; and soon after that the professor leaves a bulky document and goes into the weird hills with feverish expectancy and strange terror in his heart. He never returns, but beside a fantastic stone in the wild country are found his watch, money, and ring, done up with catgut in a parchment bearing the same terrible characters as those on the black Babylonish seal and the rock in the Welsh mountains.

The bulky document explains enough to bring up the most hideous vistas. Professor Gregg, from the massed evidence presented by the Welsh disappearances, the rock inscription, the accounts of ancient geographers, and the black seal, has decided that a frightful race of dark primal beings of immemorial antiquity and wide former diffusion still dwells beneath the hills of unfrequented Wales. Further research has unriddled the message of the black seal, and proved that the idiot boy, a son of some father more terrible than mankind, is the heir of monstrous memories and possibilities. That strange night in the study the professor invoked 'the awful transmutation of the hills' by the aid of the black seal, and aroused in the hybrid idiot the horrors of his shocking paternity. He "saw his body swell and become distended as a bladder, while the face blackened. . . ." And then the supreme effects of the invocation appeared, and Professor Gregg knew the stark frenzy of cosmic panic in its darkest form. He knew the abysmal gulfs of abnormality that he had opened, and went forth into the wild hills prepared and resigned. He would meet the unthinkable 'Little People'—and his document ends with a rational observation: "If I unhappily do not return from my journey, there is no need to conjure up here a picture of the awfulness of my fate."

Also in *The Three Impostors* is the "Novel of the White Powder", which approaches the absolute culmination of loathsome fright. Francis Leicester, a young law student nervously worn out by seclusion and overwork, has a prescription filled by an old apothecary none too careful about the state of his drugs. The substance, it later turns out, is an unusual salt which time and varying temperature have accidentally changed to something very strange and terrible; nothing less, in short, than the mediaeval *Vinum Sabbati*, whose consumption at the horrible orgies of the Witches' Sabbath gave rise to shocking transformations and—if injudiciously used—to unutterable consequences. Innocently enough, the youth regularly imbibes the powder in a glass of water after meals; and at first seems substantially benefited. Gradually, however, his improved spirits take the form of dissipation; he is absent from home a great deal, and appears to have undergone a repellent psychological change. One day an odd livid spot appears on his right hand, and he afterward returns to his seclusion; finally keeping himself shut within his room and admitting none of the household. The doctor calls for an interview, and departs in a palsy of horror, saying that he can do no more in that house. Two weeks later the patient's sister, walking outside, sees a monstrous thing at the sickroom window; and servants report that food left at the locked door is no longer touched. Summons at the door bring only a sound of shuffling and a demand in a thick gurgling voice to be let alone. At last an awful happening is reported by a shuddering housemaid. The ceiling of the room below Leicester's is stained with a hideous black fluid, and a pool of viscid abomination has dripped to the bed beneath. Dr. Haberden, now persuaded to return to the house, breaks down the young man's door and strikes again and again with an iron bar at the blasphemous semi-living thing he finds there. It is "a dark and putrid mass, seething with corruption and hideous rottenness, neither liquid nor solid, but melting and changing". Burning points like eyes shine out of its midst, and before it is despatched it tries to lift what might have been an arm. Soon afterward the physician, unable to endure the memory of what he has beheld, dies at sea while bound for a new life in America.

Mr. Machen returns to the daemoniac "Little People" in "The Red Hand" and "The Shining Pyramid"; and in *The Terror*, a wartime story, he treats with very potent mystery the effect of man's modern repudiation of spirituality on the beasts of the world, which are thus led to question his supremacy and to unite for his extermination. Of utmost delicacy, and passing from mere horror into true mysticism, is *The Great Return*, a story of the Graal, also a product of the war period. Too well known to need description here is the tale of "The Bowmen"; which, taken for authentic narration, gave rise to the widespread legend of the "Angels of Mons"—ghosts of the old English archers of Crécy and Agincourt who fought in 1914 beside the hard-pressed ranks of England's glorious "Old Contemptibles".

Less intense than Mr. Machen in delineating the extremes of stark fear, yet infinitely more closely wedded to the idea of an unreal world constantly pressing upon ours, is the inspired and prolific Algernon Blackwood, amidst whose voluminous and uneven work may be found some of the finest spectral literature of this or any age. Of the quality of Mr. Blackwood's genius there can be no dispute; for no one has even approached the skill, seriousness, and minute fidelity with which he records the overtones of strangeness in ordinary things and experiences, or the preternatural insight with which he builds up detail by detail the complete sensations and perceptions leading from reality into supernormal life or vision. Without notable command of the poetic witchery of mere words, he is the one absolute and unquestioned master of weird atmosphere; and can evoke what amounts almost to a story from a simple fragment of humourless psychological description. Above all others he understands how fully some sensitive minds dwell forever on the borderland of dream, and how relatively slight is the distinction betwixt those images formed from actual objects and those excited by the play of the imagination.

Mr. Blackwood's lesser work is marred by several defects such as ethical didacticism, occasional insipid whimsicality, the flatness of benignant supernaturalism, and a too free use of the trade jargon of modern "occultism". A fault of his more serious efforts is that diffuseness and long-windedness which results from an excessively elaborate attempt, under the handicap of a somewhat bald and journalistic style devoid of intrinsic magic, colour, and vitality, to visualise precise sensations and nuances of uncanny suggestion. But in spite of all this, the major products of Mr. Blackwood attain a genuinely classic level, and evoke as does nothing else in literature an awed and convinced sense of the immanence of strange spiritual spheres or entities.

The well-nigh endless array of Mr. Blackwood's fiction includes both novels and shorter tales, the latter sometimes independent and sometimes arrayed in series. Foremost of all must be reckoned "The Willows", in which the nameless presences on a desolate Danube island are horribly felt and recognised by a pair of idle voyagers. Here art and restraint in narrative reach their very highest development, and an impression of lasting poignancy is produced without a single strained passage or a single false note. Another amazingly potent though less artistically finished tale is "The Wendigo", where we are confronted by horrible evidences of a vast forest daemon about which North Woods lumbermen whisper at evening. The manner in which certain footprints tell certain unbelievable things is really a marked triumph in craftsmanship. In "An Episode in a Lodging House" we behold frightful presences summoned out of black space by a sorcerer, and "The Listener" tells of the awful psychic residuum creeping about an old house where a leper died. In the volume titled *Incredible Adventures* occur some of the finest tales which the author has yet produced, leading the fancy to wild rites on nocturnal hills, to secret and terrible aspects lurking behind stolid scenes, and to unimaginable vaults of mystery below the sands and pyramids of Egypt; all with a serious finesse and delicacy that convince where a cruder or lighter treatment would merely amuse. Some of these accounts are hardly stories at all, but rather studies in elusive impressions and half-remembered snatches of dream. Plot is everywhere negligible, and atmosphere reigns untrammelled.

John Silence—Physician Extraordinary is a book of five related tales, through which a single character runs his triumphant course. Marred only by traces of the popular and conventional detective-story atmosphere—for Dr. Silence is one of those benevolent geniuses who employ their remarkable powers to aid worthy fellow-men in difficulty— these narratives contain some of the author's best work, and produce an illusion at once emphatic and lasting. The opening tale, "A Psychical Invasion", relates what befell a sensitive author in a house once the scene of dark deeds, and how a legion of fiends was exorcised. "Ancient Sorceries", perhaps the finest tale in the book, gives an almost hypnotically vivid account of an old French town where once the unholy Sabbath was kept by all the people in the form of cats. In "The Nemesis of Fire" a hideous elemental is evoked by new-spilt blood, whilst "Secret Worship" tells of a German school where Satanism held sway, and where long afterward an evil aura remained. "The Camp of the Dog" is a werewolf tale, but is weakened by moralisation and professional "occultism".

Too subtle, perhaps, for definite classification as horror-tales, yet possibly more truly artistic in an absolute sense, are such delicate phantasies as *Jimbo* or *The Centaur*. Mr. Blackwood achieves in these novels a close and palpitant approach to the inmost substance of dream, and works enormous havock with the conventional barriers between reality and imagination.

Unexcelled in the sorcery of crystalline singing prose, and supreme in the creation of a gorgeous and languorous world of iridescently exotic vision, is Edward John Moreton Drax Plunkett, Eighteenth Baron Dunsany, whose tales and short plays form an almost unique element in our literature. Inventor of a new mythology and weaver of surprising folklore, Lord Dunsany stands dedicated to a strange world of fantastic beauty, and pledged to eternal warfare against the coarseness and ugliness of diurnal reality. His point of view is the most truly cosmic of any held in the literature of any period. As sensitive as Poe to dramatic values and the significance of isolated words and details, and far better equipped rhetorically through a simple lyric style based on the prose of the King James Bible, this author draws with tremendous effectiveness on nearly every body of myth and legend within the circle of European culture; producing a composite or eclectic cycle of phantasy in which Eastern colour, Hellenic form,

Teutonic sombreness, and Celtic wistfulness are so superbly blended that each sustains and supplements the rest without sacrifice of perfect congruity and homogeneity. In most cases Dunsany's lands are fabulous—"beyond the East", or "at the edge of the world". His system of original personal and place names, with roots drawn from classical, Oriental, and other sources, is a marvel of versatile inventiveness and poetic discrimination; as one may see from such specimens as "Argimenes", "Bethmoora", "Poltarnees", "Camorak", "Illuriel", or "Sardathrion".

Beauty rather than terror is the keynote of Dunsany's work. He loves the vivid green of jade and of copper domes, and the delicate flush of sunset on the ivory minarets of impossible dream-cities. Humour and irony, too, are often present to impart a gentle cynicism and modify what might otherwise possess a naive intensity. Nevertheless, as is inevitable in a master of triumphant unreality, there are occasional touches of cosmic fright which come well within the authentic tradition. Dunsany loves to hint slyly and adroitly of monstrous things and incredible dooms, as one hints in a fairy tale. In *The Book of Wonder* we read of Hlo-hlo, the gigantic spider-idol which does not always stay at home; of what the Sphinx feared in the forest; of Slith, the thief who jumps over the edge of the world after seeing a certain light lit and knowing *who* lit it; of the anthropophagous Gibbelins, who inhabit an evil tower and guard a treasure; of the Gnoles, who live in the forest and from whom it is not well to steal; of the City of Never, and the eyes that watch in the Under Pits; and of kindred things of darkness. *A Dreamer's Tales* tells of the mystery that sent forth all men from Bethmoora in the desert; of the vast gate of Perdóndaris, that was carved from a *single piece* of ivory; and of the voyage of poor old Bill, whose captain cursed the crew and paid calls on nasty-looking isles new-risen from the sea, with low thatched cottages having evil, obscure windows.

Many of Dunsany's short plays are replete with spectral fear. In *The Gods of the Mountain* seven beggars impersonate the seven green idols on a distant hill, and enjoy ease and honour in a city of worshippers until they hear that *the real idols are missing from their wonted seats*. A very ungainly sight in the dusk is reported to them—"rock should not walk in the evening"—and at last, as they sit awaiting the arrival of a troop of dancers, they note that the approaching footsteps are heavier than those of good dancers ought to be. Then things ensue, and in the end the presumptuous blasphemers are turned to green jade statues by the very walking statues whose sanctity they outraged. But mere plot is the very least merit of this marvellously effective play. The incidents and developments are those of a supreme master, so that the whole forms one of the most important contributions of the present age not only to drama, but to literature in general. *A Night at an Inn* tells of four thieves who have stolen the emerald eye of Klesh, a monstrous Hindoo god. They lure to their room and succeed in slaying the three priestly avengers who are on their track, but in the night Klesh comes gropingly for his eye; and having gained it and departed, calls each of the despoilers out into the darkness for an unnamed punishment. In *The Laughter of the Gods* there is a doomed city at the jungle's edge, and a ghostly lutanist heard only by those about to die (cf. Alice's spectral harpsichord in Hawthorne's *House of the Seven Gables*); whilst *The Queen's Enemies* retells the anecdote of Herodotus in which a vengeful princess invites her foes to a subterranean banquet and lets in the Nile to drown them.

But no amount of mere description can convey more than a fraction of Lord Dunsany's pervasive charm. His prismatic cities and unheard-of rites are touched with a sureness which only mastery can engender, and we thrill with a sense of actual participation in his secret mysteries. To the truly imaginative he is a talisman and a key unlocking rich storehouses of dream and fragmentary memory; so that we may think of him not only as a poet, but as one who makes each reader a poet as well.

At the opposite pole of genius from Lord Dunsany, and gifted with an almost diabolic power of calling horror by gentle steps from the midst of prosaic daily life, is the scholarly Montague Rhodes James, Provost of Eton College, antiquary of note, and recognised authority on mediaeval manuscripts and cathedral history. Dr. James, long fond of telling spectral tales at Christmastide, has become by slow degrees a literary weird fictionist of the very first rank; and has developed a distinctive style and method likely to serve as models for an enduring line of disciples.

The art of Dr. James is by no means haphazard, and in the preface to one of his collections he has formulated three very sound rules for macabre composition. A ghost story, he believes, should have a familiar setting in the modern period, in order to approach closely the reader's sphere of experience. Its spectral phenomena, moreover, should be malevolent rather than beneficent; since *fear* is the emotion primarily to be excited. And finally, the technical patois of "occultism" or pseudo-science ought carefully to be avoided; lest the charm of casual verisimilitude be smothered in unconvincing pedantry.

Dr. James, practicing what he preaches, approaches his themes in a light and often conversational way. Creating the illusion of every-day events, he introduces his abnormal phenomena cautiously and gradually; relieved at every turn by touches of homely and prosaic detail, and sometimes spiced with a snatch or two of antiquarian scholarship. Conscious of the close relation between present weirdness and accumulated tradition, he generally provides remote historical antecedents for his incidents; thus being able to utilise very aptly his exhaustive knowledge of the past, and his ready and convincing command of archaic diction and colouring. A favourite scene for a James tale is some centuried cathedral, which the author can describe with all the familiar minuteness of a specialist in that field.

Sly humorous vignettes and bits of life-like genre portraiture and characterisation are often to be found in Dr. James's narratives, and serve in his skilled hands to augment the general effect rather than to spoil it, as the same qualities would tend to do with a lesser craftsman. In inventing a new type of ghost, he has departed considerably from the conventional Gothic tradition; for where the older stock ghosts were pale and stately, and apprehended chiefly through the sense of sight, the average James ghost is lean, dwarfish, and hairy—a sluggish, hellish night-abomination midway betwixt beast and man—and usually *touched* before it is *seen*. Sometimes the spectre is of still more eccentric composition; a roll of flannel with spidery eyes, or an invisible entity which moulds itself in bedding and shews *a face of crumpled linen*. Dr. James has, it is clear, an intelligent and scientific knowledge of human nerves and feelings; and knows just how to apportion statement, imagery, and subtle suggestions in order to secure the best results with his readers. He is an artist in incident and arrangement rather than in atmosphere, and reaches the emotions more often through the intellect than directly. This method, of course, with its occasional absences of sharp climax, has its drawbacks as well as its advantages; and many will miss the thorough atmospheric tension which writers like Machen are careful to build up with words and scenes. But only a few of the tales are open to the charge of tameness. Generally the laconic unfolding of abnormal events in adroit order is amply sufficient to produce the desired effect of cumulative horror.

The short stories of Dr. James are contained in four small collections, entitled respectively *Ghost-Stories of an Antiquary, More Ghost Stories of an Antiquary, A Thin Ghost and Others,* and *A Warning to the Curious.* There is also a delightful juvenile phantasy, *The Five Jars,* which has its spectral adumbrations. Amidst this wealth of material it is hard to select a favourite or especially typical tale, though each reader will no doubt have such preferences as his temperament may determine.

"Count Magnus" is assuredly one of the best, forming as it does a veritable Golconda of suspense and suggestion. Mr. Wraxall is an English traveller of the middle nineteenth century, sojourning in Sweden to secure material for a book. Becoming interested in the ancient family of De la Gardie, near the village of Råbäck, he studies its records; and finds particular fascination in the builder of the existing manor-house, one Count Magnus, of whom strange and terrible things are whispered. The Count, who flourished early in the seventeenth century, was a stern landlord, and famous for his severity toward poachers and delinquent tenants. His cruel punishments were bywords, and there were dark rumours of influences which even survived his interment in the great mausoleum he built near the church—as in the case of the two peasants who hunted on his preserves one night a century after his death. There were hideous screams in the woods, and near the tomb of Count Magnus an unnatural laugh and the clang of a great door. Next morning the priest found the two men; one a maniac, and the other dead, with the flesh of his face sucked from the bones.

Mr. Wraxall hears all these tales, and stumbles on more guarded references to a *Black Pilgrimage* once taken by the Count; a pilgrimage to Chorazin in Palestine, one of the cities denounced by Our Lord in the Scriptures, and in which old priests say that Antichrist is to be born. No one dares to hint just what that Black Pilgrimage was, or what strange being or thing the Count brought back as a companion. Meanwhile Mr. Wraxall is increasingly anxious to explore the mausoleum of Count Magnus, and finally secures permission to do so, in the company of a deacon. He finds several monuments and three copper sarcophagi, one of which is the Count's. Round the edge of this latter are several bands of engraved scenes, including a singular and hideous delineation of a pursuit—the pursuit of a frantic man through a forest by a squat muffled figure with a devil-fish's tentacle, directed by a tall cloaked man on a neighbouring hillock. The sarcophagus has three massive steel padlocks, one of which is lying open on the floor, reminding the traveller of a metallic clash he heard the day before when passing the mausoleum and wishing idly that he might see Count Magnus.

His fascination augmented, and the key being accessible, Mr. Wraxall pays the mausoleum a second and solitary visit and finds another padlock unfastened. The next day, his last in Råbäck, he again goes alone to bid the long-dead Count farewell. Once more queerly impelled to utter a whimsical wish for a meeting with the buried nobleman, he now sees to his disquiet that only one of the padlocks remains on the great sarcophagus. Even as he looks, that last lock drops noisily to the floor, and there comes a sound as of creaking hinges. Then the monstrous lid appears very slowly to rise, and Mr. Wraxall flees in panic fear without refastening the door of the mausoleum.

During his return to England the traveller feels a curious uneasiness about his fellow-passengers on the canal-boat which he employs for the earlier stages. Cloaked figures make him nervous, and he has a sense of being watched and followed. Of twenty-eight persons whom he counts, only twenty-six appear at meals; and the missing two are always a tall cloaked man and a shorter muffled figure. Completing his water travel at Harwich, Mr. Wraxall takes frankly to flight in a closed carriage, but sees two cloaked figures at a crossroad. Finally he lodges at a small house in a village and spends the time making frantic notes. On the second morning he is found dead, and during the inquest seven jurors faint at sight of the body. The house where he stayed is never again inhabited, and upon its demolition half a century later his manuscript is discovered in a forgotten cupboard.

In "The Treasure of Abbot Thomas" a British antiquary unriddles a cipher on some Renaissance painted windows, and thereby discovers a centuried hoard of gold in a niche half way down a well in the courtyard of a German abbey. But the crafty depositor had set a guardian over that treasure, and something in the black well twines its arms around the searcher's neck in such a manner that the quest is abandoned, and a clergyman sent for. Each night after that the discoverer feels a stealthy presence and detects a horrible odour of mould outside the door of his hotel room, till finally the clergyman makes a daylight replacement of the stone at the mouth of the treasure-vault in the well—out of which something had come in the dark to avenge the disturbing of old Abbot Thomas's gold. As he completes his work the cleric observes a curious toad-like carving on the ancient well-head, with the Latin motto *'Depositum custodi—* keep that which is committed to thee."

Other notable James tales are "The Stalls of Barchester Cathedral", in which a grotesque carving comes curiously to life to avenge the secret and subtle murder of an old Dean by his ambitious successor; "'Oh, Whistle, and I'll Come to You, My Lad'", which tells of the horror summoned by a strange metal whistle found in a mediaeval church ruin; and "An Episode of Cathedral History", where the dismantling of a pulpit uncovers an archaic tomb whose lurking daemon spreads panic and pestilence. Dr. James, for all his light touch, evokes fright and hideousness in their most shocking forms; and will certainly stand as one of the few really creative masters in his darksome province.

For those who relish speculation regarding the future, the tale of supernatural horror provides an interesting field. Combated by a mounting wave of plodding realism, cynical flippancy, and sophisticated disillusionment, it is yet encouraged by a parallel tide of growing mysticism, as developed both through the fatigued reaction of "occultists" and religious fundamentalists against materialistic discovery and through the stimulation of wonder and fancy by such enlarged vistas and broken barriers as modern science has given us with its intra-atomic chemistry, advancing astrophysics, doctrines of relativity, and probings into biology and human thought. At the present moment the favouring forces would appear to have somewhat of an advantage; since there is unquestionably more cordiality shewn toward weird writings than when, thirty years ago, the best of Arthur Machen's work fell on the stony ground of the smart and cocksure 'nineties. Ambrose Bierce, almost unknown in his own time, has now reached something like general recognition.

Startling mutations, however, are not to be looked for in either direction. In any case an approximate balance of tendencies will continue to exist; and while we may justly expect a further subtilisation of technique, we have no reason to think that the general position of the spectral in literature will be altered. It is a narrow though essential branch of human expression, and will chiefly appeal as always to a limited audience with keen special sensibilities. Whatever universal masterpiece of tomorrow may be wrought from phantasm or terror will owe its acceptance rather to a supreme workmanship than to a sympathetic theme. Yet who shall declare the dark theme a positive handicap? Radiant with beauty, the Cup of the Ptolemies was carven of onyx.

ACKNOWLEDGEMENTS

This anthology would not exist if not for a suggestion by veteran and Lovecraft fan Matthew T. Carpenter in his review of *Worlds of H. P. Lovecraft* on Amazon. Thank you, Matthew, for that and for your service to our country.

I am indebted to S. T. Joshi for graciously providing his corrected text of *Supernatural Horror in Literature* and to Robert C. Harrall, manager of Lovecraft Holdings LLC, for permission to reprint it here.

Thanks to Gary Reed at Caliber for publishing this new edition and to Tom Mason and Dave Olbrich at Malibu Graphics for publishing the original Herbert West anthology more years ago than I care to count.

More thanks to the artists who contributed the incredible illustrations that grace this new edition.

Thanks also to my good and talented friend Justin Beahm for his foreword. It means a lot to have you be a part of this.

I am also indebted to the University of Iowa Main Library for its invaluable reference material and providing me my favorite respite sanctuary. And I would be remiss if I did not thank Professors J. Kenneth Kuntz and Jay Holstein of the university's Department of Religion for teaching me that most important of writing skills: how to read.

Finally, and always, I am most thankful to Lisa and Katie, the best and most blessed parts of my life.

BIBLIOGRAPHY

Books (Fiction)

Doyle, Sir Arthur Conan
- *The Annotated Sherlock Holmes, Vol. 1-2*, ed. Baring-Gould, William S. (Clarkson N. Potter, 1979)

Hammett, Dashiell (ed.)
- *Creeps by Night: Chills and Thrills Selected by Dashiell Hammett* (Blue Ribbon Books, 1936)

Lovecraft, H. P.
- *The Best of H. P. Lovecraft: Bloodcurdling Tales of Horror and the Macabre* (Del Rey, 1982)
- *Dagon and Other Macabre Tales* Arkham House, 1987)
- *Re-Animator: Tales of Herbert West, Six Stories by H. P. Lovecraft*, ed. Jones, Steven Philip (Malibu Graphics, 1991)

Shelley, Mary Wollstonecraft
- *Frankenstein, or The Modern Prometheus*, illustrations by Berni Wrightson (Marvel Comics Group, 1983)

Wolf, Leonard (ed.)
- *Annotated Dracula* (Potter, 1975)
- *Essential Dr. Jekyll & Mr. Hyde* (ibooks, 2005)

Books (Nonfiction)

Booth, Martin
- *The Doctor and the Detective: A Biography of Sir Arthur Conan Doyle* (St. Martin's Press, Advanced Uncorrected Proof, 1997)

Brunas, John & Michael, Weaver, Tom
- *Universal Horrors: The Studios Classic Films, 1931-1946* (McFarland Publishing, 1990)

Cannon, P.H.
- *H.P Lovecraft* (Twayne Publishers, 1989)

Fischer, Dennis
- *Horror Film Directors: 1931-1990* (McFarland Publishing, 1991)

Joshi, S.T.
- *A Dreamer and a Visionary: H. P. Lovecraft in His Time* (Liverpool University Press, 2001)
- *Call of Cthulhu and Other Weird Stories*, ed. (Penguin Books, 1999)
- *Supernatural Horror in Literature*, ed. (Hippocampus Press, 2000, 2012)

Legget, Paul
- *Terence Fisher: Horror, Myth & Religion* (McFarland Publishing, 2002)

Sampson, Robert
- *Yesterday's Faces: Vol. I, Glory Figures* (Bowling Green University Popular Press, 1983)
- *Yesterday's Faces: Vol. II, Strange Days* (Bowling Green University Popular Press, 1983)
- *Yesterday's Faces: Vol. III, From the Dark Side* (Bowling Green University Popular Press, 1983)
- *Yesterday's Faces: Vol. IV, The Solvers* (Bowling Green University Popular Press, 1983)
- *Yesterday's Faces: Vol. V, Dangerous Horizons* (Bowling Green University Popular Press, 1983)
- *Yesterday's Faces: Vol. VI, Violent Lives* (Bowling Green University Popular Press, 1983)

Comics & Graphic Novels

Jones, Steven Philip & Reed, Gary
- *Curious Cases of Sherlock Holmes* (IDW Publishing (2011)

Jones, Steven Philip
- *Re-Animator, Issues 1-3* (Adventure Comics/Malibu Graphics, 1991)
- *Worlds of H. P. Lovecraft, Vol. 1* (TransFuzion Publishing, 2008)
- *Worlds of H. P. Lovecraft, Vol. 2* (TransFuzion Publishing, 2009)

Internet Sources

The Geek Shall Inherit the Earth
- "Retro Review: Dwain Esper's *Maniac* (1934)": http://geekshallinheritearth.blogspot.com/2011/08/retro-review-dwain-espers-maniac-1934.html

Joshi, S. T.
- *The Scriptorium: "H. P. Lovecraft"*:
  http://www.themodernword.com/scriptorium/lovecraft.html

Miskatonic University
- *Periodical Reading Room: "H. P. Lovecraft in the Comics"*:
  http://www.yankeeclassic.com/miskatonic/library/stacks/periodicals/comics
  /lovecraft/comics1.htm

Wikipedia
- *Herbert West—Reanimator*:
  http://en.wikipedia.org/wiki/Herbert_West%E2%80%93Reanimator
- *Maniac (1934)*: http://en.wikipedia.org/wiki/Maniac_(1934_film)

CONTRIBUTORS

Justin Beahm is a writer, musician, actor, producer, and director. His articles on horror films, soundtracks and creators have appeared in a variety of magazines and websites including *Horror Hound*, *Famous Monsters of Filmland* and *Fangoria*. Justin's website is: http://justinbeahm.com/.

Steven Philip Jones is a writer, reviewer and editor. His most recent book is *The Clive Cussler Adventures: A Critical Review*. He has adapted several of Lovecraft's short stories into comics, and along with Christopher Jones adapted the film *Re-Animator* into comics. Steven is the creator of the original horror-adventure comics *Nightlinger* and *Vanguard*, and co-creator of the fantasy series *Talismen* with Barb Jacobs. Steve's website is: http://stevenphilipjones.com/.

S. T. (Sunand Tryambak) Joshi is a literary critic, biographer, historian and one of the leading scholars about H. P. Lovecraft. S. T. has perhaps done more than anyone to correct and champion Lovecraft's work over the last thirty years, and his work has won numerous awards including a Bram Stoker Award for Nonfiction and a World Fantasy Award for Professional Scholarship. S. T.'s website is http://stjoshi.org/.

Terry Pavlet graduated from the Milwaukee Institute of Art and Design with BFA's in Illustration, Graphic Design, and Advertising. Pavlet has created works for publications such as Print Magazine, The Society of Illustrators Annual and The Art Of H. P. Lovecraft's Cthulhu Mythos among others. Clients include Disney, Image, Wizard of the Coast, Miller Brewing, Playboy, Ballantine Books, and more. Terry's website is https://tpavlet.wordpress.com/about/.

H. P. Lovecraft is often cited as one of the three titans of American horror along with Edgar Allan Poe and Stephen King. His fiction continues to influence horror and fantasy writers while creations like Cthulhu, the Necronomicon and Herbert West have become horror icons.

INDEX

ALSO AVAILABLE FROM CALIBER COMICS

QUALITY GRAPHIC NOVELS TO ENTERTAIN

THE SEARCHERS: VOLUME 1
The Shape of Things to Come

Before *League of Extraordinary Gentlemen* there was *The Searchers*. At the dawn of the 20th Century the greatest literary adventurers from the minds of Wells, Doyle, Burroughs, and Haggard were created. All thought to be the work of pure fiction. However, a century later, the real-life descendents of those famous characters are recuited by the legendary Professor Challenger in order to save mankind's future. Series collected for the first time.

"Searchers is the comic book I have on the wall with a sign reading - 'Love books? Never read a comic? Try this one! ....money back guarantee..." - Dark Star Books.

WAR OF THE WORLDS: INFESTATION

Based on the H.G. Wells classic! The "Martian Invasion" has begun again and now mankind must fight for its very humanity. It happened slowly at first but by the third year, it seemed that the war was almost over... the war was almost lost.

"Writer Randy Zimmerman has a fine grasp of drama, and spins the various strands of the story into a coherent whole... imaginative and very gritty."
- war-of-the-worlds.co.uk

HELSING: LEGACY BORN

From writer Gary Reed (Deadworld) and artists John Lowe (Captain America), Bruce McCorkindale (Godzilla). She was born into a legacy she wanted no part of and pushed into a battle recessed deep in the shadows of the night. Samantha Helsing is torn between two worlds...two allegiances...two families. The legacy of the Van Helsing family and their crusade against the "night creatures" comes to modern day with the most unlikely of all warriors.

"Congratulations on this masterpiece..."
- Paul Dale Roberts, Compuserve Reviews

DEADWORLD

Before there was The Walking Dead there was Deadworld. Here is an introduction of the long running classic horror series, Deadworld, to a new audience! Considered by many to be the godfather of the original zombie comic with over 100 issues and graphic novels in print and over 1,000,000 copies sold, Deadworld ripped into the undead with intelligent zombies on a mission and a group of poor teens riding in a school bus desperately try to stay one step ahead of the sadistic, Harley-riding King Zombie. Death, mayhem, and a touch of supernatural evil made Deadworld a classic and now here's your chance to get into the story!

DAYS OF WRATH

Award winning comic writer & artist Wayne Vansant brings his gripping World War II saga of war in the Pacific to Guadalcanal and the Battle of Bloody Ridge. This is the powerful story of the long, vicious battle for Guadalcanal that occurred in 1942-43. When the U.S. Navy orders its outnumbered and out-gunned ships to run from the Japanese fleet, they abandon American troops on a bloody, battered island in the South Pacific.

"Heavy on authenticity, compellingly written and beautifully drawn."
- Comics Buyers Guide

THE BOBCAT

Described as the Native American *Black Panther*.
1898. Indian Territory. Will Firemaker is a Cherokee Blacksmith who is finding out that the world of ancient lore and myth of his Tribe, that Will had always thought of as tribal fairytales, are actually true, and they're telling him he must replace his best friend from the animal kingdom, The Great Cat, as the guardian of his people. This sends him down a path of shock and disbelief as beings from the ancient past begin to manifest themselves in the world of reality. And as malevolent forces rise up in the wake of the fledgling Industrial Age, the future rushes head on into the Old West. Tahlequah will never be the same...

CALIBER PRESENTS

The original Caliber Presents anthology title was one of Caliber's inaugural releases and featured predominantly new creators, many of which went onto successful careers in the comics' industry. In this new version, Caliber Presents has expanded to graphic novel size and while still featuring new creators it also includes many established professional creators with new visions. Creators featured in this first issue include nominees and winners of some of the industry's major awards including the Eisner, Harvey, Xeric, Ghastly, Shel Dorf, Comic Monsters, and more.

LEGENDLORE

From Caliber Comics now comes the entire Realm and Legendlore saga as a set of volumes that collects the long running critically acclaimed series. In the vein of The Lord of The Rings and The Hobbit with elements of Game of Thrones and Dungeon and Dragons.

Four normal modern day teenagers are plunged into a world they thought only existed in novels and film. They are whisked away to a magical land where dragons roam the skies, orcs and hobgoblins terrorize travelers, where unicorns prance through the forest, and kingdoms wage war for dominance. It is a world where man is just one race, joining other races such as elves, trolls, dwarves, changelings, and the dreaded night creatures who steal the night.

TIME GRUNTS

What if Hitler's last great Super Weapon was – Time itself! A WWII/time travel adventure that can best be described as *Band of Brothers* meets *Time Bandits*.

October, 1944. Nazi fortunes appear bleaker by the day. But in the bowels of the Wenceslas Mines, a terrible threat has emerged . . . The Nazis have discovered the ability to conquer time itself with the help of a new ominous device!

Now a rag tag group of American GIs must stop this threat to the past, present, and future . . . While dealing with their own past, prejudices, and fears in the process.

www.calibercomics.com

www.ingramcontent.com/pod-product-compliance
Lightning Source LLC
Chambersburg PA
CBHW081328090726
47907CB00010B/2408